JANET

Janet Davey was born in 1953. She is the author of
English Correspondence, which was longlisted for
the 2002 Orange Prize, *First Aid*, *The Taxi Queue*
and *By Battersea Bridge*.

ALSO BY JANET DAVEY

English Correspondence
First Aid
The Taxi Queue
By Battersea Bridge

JANET DAVEY

Another Mother's Son

VINTAGE

1 3 5 7 9 10 8 6 4 2

Vintage
20 Vauxhall Bridge Road,
London SW1V 2SA

Vintage is part of the Penguin Random House
group of companies whose addresses can be found at
global.penguinrandomhouse.com

Penguin
Random House
UK

Copyright © Janet Davey 2015

Janet Davey has asserted her right to be identified as the
author of this Work in accordance with the Copyright,
Designs and Patents Act 1988

First published in Vintage in 2016
First published in hardback by Chatto & Windus in 2015

A CIP catalogue record for this book is available
from the British Library

ISBN 9781784701123

Printed and bound by Clays Ltd, St Ives Plc

Penguin Random House is committed to a sustainable future
for our business, our readers and our planet. This book is made
from Forest Stewardship Council® certified paper.

To Tom Cary

1

A wall is down and a small room, the receptionists' sanctum, has been exposed. Red-and-white striped barrier tape cordons off the area. Polythene sheeting, thick with peppery plaster dust, lies under a work platform of ladders and planks. Light fittings dangle from wires. Homely objects, previously glimpsed through the hatch – an electric kettle, the more comfortable chair – have been removed. There is nothing to peer at and I suppose the bell to summon will have been discarded too.

I check my phone for messages and, since I am alone, put on some lipstick, mouthing at myself in the make-up mirror. A vanity project, I think, as I snap it shut. They cut drama from the curriculum and tart up the foyer.

Although I have attended school meetings and dos for the last ten years on behalf of one son or another, I have no grasp of the layout of Lloyd-Barron Academy and often get lost. The main school, an Edwardian building, flanked by two 1960s modernist slabs, debouches into annexes that were constructed from the cheapest available materials and named after water birds – Grebe, Shearwater,

Bittern, and so on – for no known reason. The arrangement of these additions accords with no topological sense. I start from the front entrance and, via changes of level, abrupt turns and sudden plunges into open air, follow the wrong person along corridors of lino worn shiny by wear and end up in a cul-de-sac; a science prep room or a claustrophobic, bleach-scented anteroom to a set of lavatories.

A sudden rise in the temperature, a September surprise after a lousy summer, has caught me wearing the wrong clothes: black / 10 per cent Lycra / long-sleeved. A bath or shower would have been welcome but then I would have wondered what to put on in order to look as if it were a fluke that I am here at all – a last-minute decision to attend the sixth-form social evening – since part of me sides with the parents who fail to turn up on these occasions from ineptitude or sheer lack of interest. By the time I reach the sixth-form block, I am fanning myself with the evening newspaper.

They are full of goodwill, the parents who turn up at these school events, though this does not preclude whingeing. I wait for the pen to be free and write 'Ross Doig' on one of the blank labels provided, then add 'Lorna Parry' in brackets. My T-shirt is too tightly stretched for the pin so I re-fasten the label round the

2

strap of my bag from where it immediately slides down out of sight.

'Here we are again,' a father says, as I approach the refreshments table. 'Seems like ten minutes since we were doing this for Jacob and Oliver.'

'Yes, doesn't it? How is Jacob?' I take a ready-poured cup of black tea and slop milk into it from a stainless-steel jug.

I cannot remember the first name of the man who has come up to me, though I must once have been told. His label, wonkily attached to a well-darned crew-necked jumper, says 'Nina Levine'. We are all our children's parents. He is a tall bear of a man with a neatly trimmed beard and spectacles mended with a flesh-coloured plaster. He strikes me as more normal than some of the dads.

'I've no idea.' Nina Levine's father takes a gulp from his glass of red wine and grimaces. 'God almighty, the wine doesn't get any better, does it? Oh, you're drinking tea. Wise choice. No, we never hear from him. He's out in Guatemala. Been there since term ended. My wife goes on Facebook to check that he's in the land of the living. Ah! There he is. Just spotted him. Hi, Jacob. Good to see you.' He waves at a film projected onto a section of wall of the sixth-form common room. It shows students from the cohort which left in the summer and is already tinged with nostalgia. The soundtrack is switched off and the students in their white shirts and black trousers or skirts take part in noiseless discussions and conduct silent lab experiments. Teachers open and close their mouths. Chairs move as though lubricated. It is a fluid world that travels from sequence to sequence without strain – though the young people who are part of it seem vulnerable, as if on the brink of disaster.

The real-life boys and girls who hang about in small groups or perch on tables, fondling their phones, scent the air with cheap perfume and the gutsy, animal smell of their bodies. They are noisier and more brazen than those on screen. They might cope with life – not because they are stronger or more intelligent but through a plodding pedestrianism that, while not getting them far, should keep them safe. In home clothes ('mufti' so-called by the head) – drop-down jeans for the boys and various tight tops, little dresses, skinny jeans and leggings for the girls – they seem set fair for whatever might come their way, whether gap years, university, or NEET: the current limbo, or purgatory, of being in neither education, employment nor training.

'Oliver's away at Porthkerris in Cornwall,' I say. 'Night diving this time. My father paid for him to have lessons. He feels the lure of the ocean. He carries on wanting things, of course – wetsuit, masks, fins, BCDs, whatever they are, the latest pieces of electronic kit. Money, money, money. An ever-rolling stream.'

4

'At least they didn't have gap years. What are they *for*? Private-school kids have them, don't they? On the whole, I disapprove. They're a hybrid of finishing school and a bloody long holiday.'

'It would be more of an adventure to ditch the mobile and go to Rotherham and live with a landlady.'

Nina's father guffaws. 'They conform. That's probably the sole point. You've got a third son, haven't you? Still at uni, is he? How's he doing?'

'Ewan? He's OK. Trundling along.'

My companion sloshes the wine around in his glass, getting a small eddy going into which he stares. 'It's a shame Miss Bhimji left. She was great. Ross is doing English, isn't he?'

'Yup. I don't know who they've got. Ross doesn't speak to me.'

'Alan Child, apparently. Nina says he's been here a year. This will be his first go with the sixth form. They like to give the young staff a turn. Watch the results go down. Could that be him?' He indicates a man standing alone in front of the lockers.

'He's the right age. Too young to be an Alan, don't you think? I wonder whether he has adopted the name to give himself gravitas in the staffroom. He doesn't look overly inspiring, does he? A bit of a tit? He keeps rolling his shoulders. Oh dear. I hope he's not going to take time off for physiotherapy. The jacket's too big for him. It slips about like a borrowed silk dressing gown.'

'Enough, Lorna! You're as bad as Nina. Well, I suppose we'd better mingle. Meet the teachers. That's what we're here for, isn't it?' Nina's father grins and shambles away.

Groups are beginning to cluster around individual members of staff. Unworldly Mrs Anstey with her grey hair loose about her shoulders and floor-length wrap-around skirt. Mr Frost, whose bloodshot eyes become more vacant with every year that passes. Though the occasion is billed as social, and it is less than two weeks into the new term, parents cannot stop themselves from lining up and asking about Harry's progress. Douglas Milner, head of sixth form and pastoral mainstay, has been trapped by Deborah Lupton. She talks and gesticulates while he nods slowly above her, his wine glass empty. The older members of staff are teachers through and through. Line them up in an identity parade and anyone would guess their profession. It is all those days of virtual imprisonment without the opportunity to pop out to the shops, breathe fresh air or go for a decent lunch. Schools are, more often than not, away from society, at the far end of long, meandering roads, served by only one bus. They have this in common with municipal cemeteries. To whatever teachers suffer in the way of a commute can be added this extra leg that takes them from a recognisable landscape through increasingly surreal terrain that seems to go on for miles. Somehow it affects the psyche. They become different people from the ones who set out.

Grace Lu's mother has taken up a position behind the refreshments table and is serving coffee. She belongs to the inner circle of parents who take part in fund-raising activities. They know each other and understand the urn.

'Sorry. The chocolate biscuits have all gone,' she says.

Another mother finds this sublimely funny and bursts out laughing.

2

The engine is running and the passenger door wide open. Ross hops from foot to foot on the driver's side and makes signs to me to open the window.

'For God's sake, Ross, just get in. Where were you all evening?'

At one point, I saw him walking aimlessly between the display boards but failed to nab him. In his school uniform, he stood out among the mufti-wearers. 'Are you coping, man?' his friend Hunter called out, his teeth embedded in a sandwich. When I signalled to Ross that I was keen to leave he held up a hand, fingers spread, and mouthed that he would meet me in the car park in five. He wandered out again through a different door. I waited in the car, listening without much attention to a medical programme on Radio 4 about a link between taking sleeping pills and early death.

Ross leans forward as the window slides down. 'Mum, is it all right if I go home with Jude?'

He peers in at me. He can be polite when he wants something, stubborn as the lid of a vacuum-sealed jar for the rest of the time. It still comes as a surprise that his face above the loosened collar and skewed school tie is no longer round and chubby – though he can put on the unblinking stare of childhood at will. The arc of one eyebrow is visible, the other masked by a mop of reddish fair hair the size of a small cauliflower. With head shaved to the back and sides, he is growing out his former hedgehog haircut selectively.

'No, it isn't all right. It's a school night. Tuesday. What's the matter with you?'

'We've got this project.' His voice is adolescent husky.

'And?'

'We're supposed to do it in pairs.' He steps back from the car and looks over his shoulder.

'Well, make a start on it at the weekend.'

His face looms in the window frame again. 'That's too late, Mum. We need a working plan by tomorrow morning.'

'Do it by phone.'

'No-o.' Ross sounds anguished. 'We need to discuss and Jude's got all this good stuff.'

'Who is this supposed to be for?' I ask.

'Mr Chi-ald. That's the trouble.'

'Mr Child.' I sigh. 'I met him briefly. He seems—'

'Thanks, Mum. See you tomorrow.'

I stare into the space he had occupied. I have never

heard of Jude. He must be new. There are always fresh faces in Year 12. Lloyd-Barron Academy recruits vigorously for its sixth form. 'Specialising in Success' is the slogan.

In the driver's mirror, I have an obscure view through the sloping glass of the back windscreen to the cars lined up behind. Here and there streams of light appear as engines and headlamps are switched on. Among them is a car containing Ross and Jude and driven by one of Jude's parents. Alternatively, the story is a pack of lies and my son will shortly be a missing person.

Using repeater triangulation, we locate Ross's mobile number in a rural area in the West Midlands. Since then there has been no roaming signal. That will be £2,000 plus VAT. Please try the repeater triangulation again. Where are the rural areas in the West Midlands?

His photo will appear, smudged and out of focus, on the back pages of the *Big Issue*. Ross never stands still long enough to get a clear print. Like a ballboy on a tennis court, he is poised, ready to move. He is seventeen, not an especially grown-up seventeen; one of the oldest in his year group, which some studies suggest is an educational advantage, though I have yet to see proof of this. He is slighter than Ewan and Oliver were at that age – more of an urchin – but, I assume, capable of looking after himself. I am disinclined to cosset my boys. I have never been a taxi service. All the same, it is odd that I have no idea where and with whom he will be spending the night. The catchment area for Lloyd-Barron Academy is large and extends northwards into the Enfield suburbs as far as the M25.

Having thought that Ross's decision not to wear home clothes was a non-conformity-in-conformity thing, I now realise that he planned to stay away and purposely kept his school uniform on in order to wear it on Wednesday morning. I should have kept saying no. 'No, no, no' to everything he said. Instead I said, 'Mr Child.'

I lean across the empty passenger seat and shut the door. I switch on the headlamps and ease the car forward.

3

The lights are off when I return home. I bump against the cardboard cartons that stand stacked in the narrow hall and set a clock inside chiming. I put my bag down. The day's warmth is trapped inside the walls.

This house used to feel like a moving boat when the boys ran in and out of rooms and up and down the stairs. These days it is becalmed. I go up to the half landing, then to the first floor, switching on lights along the way. My sons keep their bedroom doors shut. They close them when they are in situ and also when they leave. The woodwork, defaced by old torn-off stickers in shards of colour, resembles the site of a butterfly massacre. The walls are pitted by missiles launched from catapults.

I continue up to Ewan's room at the top of the house. I do this every day. I appear in the converted loft and tell him bits of news – though I sound to myself like a broadcaster reading from an autocue. If he does not instantly tell me to go away, I wander about, pick up wet towels from the floor, lower or raise the blind, depending on the time of day. I venture as far as the desk and look to see if he has been drawing; adding to the strange, painstaking, intricate designs, spoiled from the start by being executed in biro. I touch his hair.

I no longer ask, Why don't you . . .? Wouldn't it be a good idea to . . .? What's the matter? How can I help? Frequently asked questions that are as useless as the kind dreamt up by some minor marketing person for a product website.

I push the door open. Ewan is a mound in the bed. From where I stand, the cocoon of duvet conceals even the top of his head.

'Hi, darling. Are you OK? Whew! It's hot in here under the roof. Surely you don't need the duvet on. Shall I fetch you a sheet? Crazy weather. Cold and wet all summer and now baking in September. Have you had anything to eat?' I pause. 'Well, the sixth-form do was boring, as expected, and your brother has disappeared into the night with someone called Jude. Fingers crossed he reappears one day. Oh, since he's not here, you could sleep in his room – or in Oliver's. It will be cooler down there. Why don't you do that?'

My words are normal, the tone bright but less bright than I intend. Too monotonous – too plangent. I am like a musician who becomes note perfect but ceases to breathe life into the sound she makes.

I go down the stairs and along the passage to the kitchen, through the door frame with its jagged gaps where the hinges used to be. I removed the door years ago to stop the interminable banging.

A lamp stands on the sill among dog-eared paper-backs with the shade touching its reflection in the window. I switch it on. Nothing in the house keeps its own space. Objects overlap like memos on a crowded noticeboard.

I write a text to Ross: This must not happen again. I erase it and send: Where are you?

I open the fridge door and look inside, shut it again. The bread bin contains half a granary loaf. I take two slices and slot them into the toaster.

There have been too many parts to the day, each element differentiated and with its own particular hue. All they have in common is myself – and that is not enough to bind them together. On the contrary, my presence obstructs the flow. Deborah Lupton bounces along full of good cheer. She sutures the lives of the twins, the younger Luptons and Mr Lupton, the Lloyd-Barron Academy Parents' Association, the drop-in centre for the over seventies, the Woodcraft Folk – and in the process makes a seamless whole of her own life. Ginny Lu, in a quieter way, is the same. These women are not merely good sorts, they are organising principles. The episodes that make up their days and weeks, whatever the contents, are all stamped by the Lupton/Lu in-house franking machine whereas I scrabble around guessing the correct postage for each and every item. When I get it wrong I imagine a scrawl across the outside of the package indicating the insufficiency or a recommendation that the mail be returned to sender.

I still see myself as a student type, a kind of girl hoodlum, though, apart from the tattoo of a snail shell on my left shoulder and the naturally back-combed hair, that notion hardly stands up. Some wised-up friend said I looked like Patty Hearst and, once I had found out who Patty Hearst was, it pleased me to be linked to someone who had been kidnapped by an urban guerrilla group and taken part in a San Francisco bank robbery. A London girl with a short upper lip and wide-apart eyes, I liked the conjured-up image of glamorous instability and, before the days of Wikipedia, went to the trouble of looking up Stockholm syndrome.

I have an ex-husband, Randal Doig, and an insecure job working as an archivist in the Corporate Archives of Transport for London. I am the mother of three sons. We live together in Dairyman's Road, Palmers Green, in a thirties house with small-paned bay windows up and down, red tiles and a roof light, invisible from the street, that looks slantwise up to the sky.

In my lunch hour, in fine weather, I lie on the grass in St James's Park. The sun feels the same on my skin as it did when I was nineteen, my eyes shut behind a pair of sunglasses.

The toaster emits a sooty smell and switches itself off. The popping-up mechanism has not worked since Ross forced in a whole hot cross bun. I look around for the meat skewer.

4

My sons were all born during John Major's government and I often wonder whether that has had an effect on them. The privatisation of British Rail, the introduction of Sunday trading, the Dangerous Dogs Act, the Cones Hotline, Back to Basics – the tone of that administration seeped into their minds and made them obstructive. As a predictor, someone's birth prime minister must be as good as an astrological sign. *Bonar Law 1922–3: Renowned for your excellent memory and business acumen, you may be depressed at losing your grip. Don't worry. Soon you will be ready for the next step. Try growing a moustache.*

Liz Savaris, my best schoolfriend, who now lives in Aberystwyth, does not think much of my theory. Birthwise, we both scraped into Alec Douglas-Home's term of office and so far have not come up with any points of reference, though *The Way the Wind Blows*, the title of A.D.-H.'s autobiography, is sufficiently fatalistic to suit most circumstances. Certainly, my own life has seen the odd twister. I call Liz whenever I need to clamour for sympathy, which she gives wholeheartedly in a real crisis but hardly at all up until that point. I rely on her, in a sense, to gauge the severity of a situation and am almost pleased to be put down because it means that, according to Liz, I am making a fuss about nothing. All kinds of awful things have happened to her and, although she never brings them up in conversation, they hover like warning angels as I prattle on.

Have you started dating? she asked when Ewan gave up university after two terms. Sometimes boys don't like that. Well, there was Richard Watson but . . . Richard Watson, she shrieked, have you gone mad, Lorna? It's either someone you already know, or a stranger, I said. Both have their pluses and minuses. He works at the Office for Budget Responsibility. But Richard Watson? she said. Ewan wouldn't have known, I said, unless he was a fly on the wall of The Albert in Victoria Street or Richard's grim flat off Fulham Palace Road. Another explanation might be the birth of Stefan, Liz said, referring to my ex-husband's new son. This has all happened so bloody fast – gestation like rats – though the baby would mainly affect Ross, as he is the one who has lost his position. Ewan is still the firstborn. We would have gone off the rails among our own age group, I said. Universities tolerate time-wasters and they have their own counselling services. Why has he come *home*?

The middle son, too drunk on the dark and the mystery of the sea to reply to his mother's messages, or just too drunk, returns from Cornwall in time for me to drive him to Brighton for the start of Freshers' Week. The journey passes without much conversation. Oliver listens to music, and I, who dislike the A23, concentrate on the road. He sits with the passenger seat pushed back in semi-recline. From my sit-up-and-beg position, I see mainly his legs, the tear in his jeans at the knee, and his thumbs as they move over his phone. The clouds are high and grey and gusts of wind buffet the side of the car with hollow sounding thuds.

At one point, Oliver starts talking about wreck tours off the south coast, then, as suddenly as he began, he replaces the earpiece under a lock of blond hair and falls silent again. This leads me to believe that his mind is on diving and that starting university is an irrelevance and not in any way momentous to him. Only time will tell whether he too will return home before or after graduation and live in his bedroom.

As far as I know, Oliver has no girlfriend. He hangs out with a group of friends, and who within that group is paired off with whom I have no idea. He is free. He won't be making those complicated weekend train journeys that Ben Allardyce and I went in for, having ended up in mutually inaccessible university towns. We used to

19

go on three-and-a-half-hour journeys from Colchester to Nottingham, or Nottingham to Colchester, via two quite separate London terminals and sometimes Grantham as well.

I keep my thoughts to myself. They come and go, like traffic flow. It feels peaceful to be in the car occasionally smacked by the wind, Oliver beside me, the tinny beat from his music a constant accompaniment.

London suburban landscape repeats itself. Detached, mansion-sized roadside pubs with banner advertisements for Sunday roast, garden centres flanked by banks of shopping trolleys, superstores, ditto. Glimpsed country-side vanishes as fast as the good parts of dreams. I sing at one point because we are on the road and moving but Oliver catches sight of my lips and gestures to me to cut it out.

We drive towards the South Downs but instead of speeding on towards the sea – the desire for which is quickened by the sight of the coastal hills rising in a long, grey-green line – we turn eastwards at the Patcham inter-change, head for the Brighton suburb of Coldean and arrive at the university campus at around midday.

I park the car while Oliver collects a key from the site manager of the halls of residence. As I wait for him to return, I smile at a couple who are lifting a television from the back of their people-carrier while their son yells instructions. More items are removed from the boot. A small fridge, a microwave oven, a rail of clothes. Shadows appear on the tarmac, generous splashes of black, as the sun breaks through cloud.

A girl poses with wide-apart arms and an open-mouthed Hollywood smile by the entrance to the block. Her father aims his phone at her. Another family stands by, luggage piled up beside them, waiting their turn for the celebrity shoot. Out come the phones and cameras. There is something sick-making about photography.

5

A single bed, desk and cupboard, all of the same blonde imitation wood, are arranged along the length of two walls and stand on a mottled brown carpet. Like a hotel bedroom, Room 8 offers a blank page on which unconnected strangers can write. I feel overwhelmed by everything that might happen to Oliver here and also by the dullness of dull student days. I put down the bags I am carrying and go over to the square, metal-framed window that overlooks the car park.

A middle-aged man trundles two vast suitcases along the paving, his paunch thrust into prominence by the backward drag. The suitcase wheels make a noise like horses clopping in rhythm until they collide. He stops to unlock them, then sets off again. A girl follows. She struggles with an armful of garments, some loose, some enclosed in plastic covers that balloon in the breeze.

'Are there enough days in the term to wear all those clothes?' I say.

I turn round and see a tall youth wearing my son's grey marl fleece and blue jeans. He is hunched over his phone. Sun-bleached hair flops forwards. He is oblivious to his surroundings. Neither man nor boy, he is in some significant way nothing to do with me, though Oliver's possessions are everywhere – his backpack and bags on the floor, his parka flung on the bed.

The front door bangs again and on the other side of the wall something clatters to the ground. 'Da-ad. Help me.'

'She's dropped the lot,' Oliver says and the slip-sliding youth vanishes.

'I hope it won't be too noisy living so close to the entrance,' I say. 'Drunken revellers. People knocking on the window if they've lost their key. I remember—'

Oliver interrupts. 'It doesn't make any difference. They're just rooms.'

This is the case. I am struck by his attitude – and proud of it – though aware that the realism is caused more by his attachment to his phone than by the taking up of a considered philosophical position. One day, the external world and the inner world will vanish, replaced by a series of beeps.

'What do you want to do?' I try out the lighting; open and shut cupboards and drawers. Raw dust of cut chipboard has settled in crevices. I pick out a long dark hair from a drawer and drop it in the wastepaper basket.

'I dunno. Unpack. See who's around.'

'What about eating? Shall we go into town and find some lunch?'

'No, it's all right. You go home if you like.'

'Really? You must be hungry, aren't you? We could get fish and chips and brave the beach.'

He shakes his head.

'Let's go and find the kitchen,' I say. 'Case the joint.'

'What? Oh, it'll be obvious.'

I think of my own mother placing a potted scented geranium on the windowsill of my first room at university, the one that looked out onto a brick wall. Later, she folded up the drab bedcover and hid it in a cupboard.

'OK, then. I may as well go,' I say.

It is only after I have slung my bag over my shoulder and stand dangling the car keys that Oliver comes to and registers what is happening. 'You leaving, Mum?' He appears perplexed. He puts his phone in the back pocket of his jeans.

'We could—'

'I'll see you off.'

I take a last look at the room. I imprint it on my mind for future reference. On the way out, I stoop and pick up a flyer that had been pushed under the door. 'CEOs and Corporate Hoes,' it says. 'Come and get raped!' The accompanying line drawing shows a be-suited man with his hand splayed over one of the spherical breasts that

24

tumbles out of a girl's low-cut top. Two champagne flutes brimming with bubbles complete the picture.

'Charming,' I say, flapping the paper at Oliver. 'Women's emancipation was for this? We're heading back to the Palaeolithic era. You should report it.'

'Don't worry about it, Mum. It's just fun.'

We leave the building and make our way between the parked vehicles, Oliver a few paces behind me. When we reach the car I open the boot to check that nothing has been left behind. I turn to Oliver and stretch out my arms for a hug. The goodbye is over. I get in the car, start the engine and reverse between the two large, shiny cars on either side. Oliver stands and watches. As the wheels go forward again, I see him in the rear-view mirror. He is waving; a side-to-side arm wave that would be visible from a departing cruise ship.

I head for London, aware of rain clouds coming from the west and the first drops on the windscreen. The South Downs shrink when approached from the south. Fast cars streak past, their engine noise amplified, trapped between hills. High above, a group of ramblers – tiny figures in brightly coloured cagoules – cross the road bridge. I fiddle with the radio and fail to get a signal. I know what I am going back to. It's as if Ewan hates what's out there, Randal, my ex-husband, said on one occasion. Out where? The world. What? As it is today;

to some extent, you hate it. You make no bones about it. Certain aspects, yes, I agreed. Are you blaming me? You're quite negative, Lorna, Randal said. Thanks, I said. Where are you in all this?

6

I should never have mentioned the three poses to Randal. It was a joke, really. Our son, Ewan, sits, head bent, with the angled lamp casting a tight circle of light onto the desk; or, in the same circle of light, with his head resting on his arms; or he lies, a mound in the bed.

For Christ's sake, Lorna, Randal said. Are you suggesting that Ewan deliberately arranges himself in one of these tableaux whenever he hears you coming upstairs? OK, I said. Let's leave it. I was trying for humour. You are, Randal said. I am what? When I come to the house you are, let's say, by the stove, by the sink, or getting stuff out of the washing machine. Thanks, I said. I'm doing all this on my own, don't forget. I always was, even when we lived together. When I came into the front room you were sitting on the sofa sanding the hard skin off your feet. It doesn't prove anything beyond my failure to prick your sluggish conscience. I only did that once, Randal said. Just once and there was a good reason. I was about to run a half-marathon. Where's your father when you go to see him on Saturday? In his chair, I replied. Exactly,

Randal said. That's just how people are; boring and predictable. We are copies of ourselves.

He did not convince me. There is more to language than words. Ewan could be saying something to me, though I have no idea what.

I last saw my ex-husband at the beginning of the summer holidays. He was wearing a black V-necked jumper over bare flesh and had grown a millimetre of beard. Same eyes, prominent and stary, with white parts that have stayed clear as he grows older, not bloodshot, nor wobbly, like just set albumen. I watch out for signs of ageing in him. The blue is changeable in colour like spilt petrol on a dark surface. He pressed his face against the glass in the front door and tripped over the loose section of matting on the stairs, as usual. Nothing was said, and yet, afterwards – after he had gone – I felt lonely, as if I had to cope with Ewan on my own. Without being able to identify any palpable signs, I sensed that Randal had begun to distance himself from the problem. The something-must-be-done desperation that afflicted him when Ewan first took up residence in his bedroom had vanished, together with the camaraderie. It was the loneliness that alerted me.

I am back in Dairyman's Road by mid-afternoon. The house is stuck at an earlier hour. The sun has moved round and falls like a golden highway across the remains of breakfast. Ross is at Jude's. I begin to clear up. I have come back too soon. I should have gone to the sea, walked along the front as far as the beach huts, sat on the sloping shingle. Instead I am in Palmers Green, slotting spoons into the cutlery basket of the dishwasher, and will shortly go to visit my father. Saturday tea at the Winchmore Hill flat, Sunday lunch at Dairyman's Road. This is what happens at weekends.

I go upstairs. Up the main flight. Up the space-saver steps. I knock gently and push the door open. The blind over the roof light is down and the room in semi-darkness, lit by the desk lamp.

Ewan's head rests on his arms, his face is hidden. The whiteness of the nape of his neck is exposed by the halogen glow. His hair spills onto his sleeve. He makes no response to the news that Oliver is installed in his student accommodation. Standing in the doorway, I move on to some other subject. He raises his head and makes some kind of reply. I am queen of the banal in my dispatches to Ewan. Luckily, I have a surplus of inconsequential thoughts. I try to avoid subjects that have a bearing on his situation. He set off, like Oliver, and then returned. It is amazing how much might, at a tangent, wound him in some way. I start on something and realise that hidden within is an implied criticism or a reminder of what he is missing.

7

Hello Lorna, Hope all is well with you and the boys. Is Ollie having fun in Brighton? JFP back from Malaysia – 'hilarious' as ever. Got the B team to do an 'egg drop' i.e. drop an egg safely from the roof using drinking straws and masking tape. Cluck, cluck, Whoa! Currently snowed under but should see the light of day in a week or so. R xx

Randal Doig, my ex-husband, works for the British subsidiary of a North American precision-engineering company based in South Cambridgeshire. He started there about four years ago – met Charmian. That was his line and he sticks to it, though I believe a back story exists and a degree of plotting. Speedy boarding, Liz calls it, because he was present at the gate and ready to go. I have never really known what he does but the company makes, or rather finds, custom-engineered something something something equipment solutions. I have tried to memorise the phrase and believe it contains the word 'rotating'. He moved out of our house in Dairyman's Road and into a rented cottage in a North Hertfordshire village that he and Charmian subsequently purchased. He comes to see the boys less frequently now and, apart from his calls from the immediate vicinity, no longer communicates by phone. He has embraced the voiceless media and sends us what are effectively round robins, alive with links to YouTube clips. As the messages sometimes contain work gossip, I guess they also go out to former colleagues who have cleared their desks and decamped. Randal is kind enough to personalise the odd sentence – usually at the beginning and again to close – and these leap out as though in a completely different font, say, Aharoni, in a lake of Tahoma.

Although I am grateful for the crumb of recognition, I feel a crisis of identity followed by hatred and reply to his latest email with the opening sentences of *Wuthering Heights*.

> *Hello Randal, I have just returned from a visit to my landlord – the solitary neighbour that I shall be troubled with. This is certainly a beautiful country! In all England I do not believe that I could have fixed on a situation so completely removed from the stir of society.*
> *Lorna*

Randal will skim read and delete.

In the centre of London, I am as quiet as a hermit. I

31

tune out tourists and marching soldiers, the State Opening of Parliament, the self-important outriders with whistles. The room I occupy is carved out of a corner of a larger one. It has an internal window, half-masked by a Venetian blind with wonky slats that looks onto the main office. Since the window is behind my desk not much looking takes place. I treat it as an aberrant part of the wall. Light comes from overhead fluorescent tubes and some, in the form of daylight, through my open door.

I work alone for much of the time, though there are volunteers at the archive and also members of the public who come by appointment to do their own research. In the last round of spending cuts, funding for extra projects was withdrawn and all the young temporary cataloguers were laid off. The big office is empty and the computers covered over. The concealed forms and dusty surfaces, together with tired paintwork, make it a place of abandonment. It might be a garment factory in abeyance through lack of orders – all stitching suspended. More than half the operations have moved out to new premises on the Greenwich Peninsula. The entire 1920s structure, the cruciform block that rises in steps to a tower above St James's Park underground station, is to be sold off and converted into bespoke luxury apartments. Civic offices, hospitals, magistrates' courts, police stations, libraries – buildings with a function throughout London – have become savings accounts with en-suite bathrooms. By night, the stairwells of these unoccupied premises are vertical bands of light. Windows glint blackly. No one lives behind them.

Every day, enquiries land in my inbox. They are often about relatives who were employed by London Transport but I also receive less mainstream requests. I form a picture of my correspondents from their names and the style of their messages; a picture that disappears rapidly as soon as I clap eyes on them. Not only are the specifics wrong but the whole tone of the person. I sometimes wonder what becomes of these images and whether they people my night-time dreams. Certainly, my dreams are full of individuals I do not know from Adam. It is no different with Chris Orrick whom I collect from reception. He turns out to be bald and agile, a retired operations manager in a freight-haulage company and, he takes pains to inform me, still available as a consultant. I loathe the newly retired. They have a life-time of work behind them and a pension and continue to forage for employment. Chris is an ambiguous name and this person might have been a woman, though the '*Cheers*' made a man more likely. He wears jeans and a red polo shirt and carries a beige mac over his arm. He has a laptop in a case, a stubby fold-up umbrella and a Marks and Spencer's plastic bag that he tells me contains a snack.

I've moved goods all over the world. Logistics have a universal resonance. Now I've retired, I want to write a novel. Nothing too dark. A London Underground disaster would make a good starting point. Cheers, Chris

I explained in my return message the difficulties of calling up unspecific material and recommended that Chris find a topic to focus on. He then homed in on the Bethnal Green crush of 1943, saying it had potential. The lapidary writing style misled me. Chris Orrick talks non-stop. His eyes go everywhere. He has never felt fitter. His contemporaries veg out on sunshine holidays but he, Chris Orrick, has a project. As we walk side by side along the corridors of closed doors, he comments on the cabling that bulges from a broken section of trunking, the high-pitched noise of a lift held open while cartons are unloaded, a missing carpet tile. The first time he halts mid-step, I think he has suddenly realised he has left something on the train, or is meant to be somewhere else. But it is to point out a defect he has spotted. 'A a a a a a a,' he says, as if he is imitating a motor scooter stuttering to a start, followed by a long low 'whoo' like wind in a ventilator.

'The place is falling apart,' I tell him. 'Nothing's been done because the block is being sold to developers. It's a wonderful building. There were once marble drinking fountains on every floor – supplied by an artesian well.'

'OK. Interesting. I remember the old drinking fountains. Filthy, weren't they? We had one in the local playground. My mother told us not to lick the metal.' He gives me a sidelong glance. 'Funny when you think about it. Little tongues poking out into an arch of water. Why would you want fountains in a place like this? Legionnaires. It's a risk. You could make a nice fitness suite down here, though.'

Speculation on the likely price per square metre of the prospective apartments accompanies us the rest of the way. By the time we reach my office, Chris Orrick is abominating social housing quotas on new-builds and recommending that I read Ayn Rand. This is fairly typical of members of the public. Right-wing views and sexual innuendo bubble out of them.

'Where's the library, then?' he says.

I explain that there are no documents on the premises. Everything is off-site in a salt mine at Winsford, Cheshire, and delivered on request.

'Wow. Any chance of a visit?' he says.

'Sorry,' I say with a polite smile. 'Staff only.'

I sit Chris Orrick at a desk. After half an hour he is still chatting. I re-park him in the main office at one of the tables. I shall no longer be able to see him but I take the risk that he is not a pyromaniac or a paper-tearer. 'No drinks, no food,' I remind him, as I glare at the Marks and Spencer's plastic bag. 'Only pencils allowed. I have my own work to get on with,' I say firmly.

He raises his eyebrows in a jocular way. 'A bit brighter by the window, isn't it? Wouldn't *you* rather be in here? I thought this research would take months but it looks like I'll polish it off in a couple of goes. There's not much information, is there?' He taps the thin folder of documents, as he re-settles himself.

'That's all we have. The press wasn't allowed to report on the tragedy. You'll find more in the Tower Hamlet's archive – eyewitness accounts and so on.'

'This writing game is a mindset thing. I've figured out how it works. You need action and you need a cracking opening to wake people up. Three hundred men and women piled on top of each other in the narrow stairwell at Bethnal Green station. What's it like to fight for your breath?' Chris Orrick clamps his hands over his nostrils and mouth. His eyes bulge and I notice small, reddish-brown discolorations in the irises.

Christ, I think.

8

My friend Liz tells me that the nuclear family is a recent invention and that children in the past were frequently farmed out to aunts and uncles, real or nominal. Having many years ago read the book from which Liz gleaned this theory, I believe that the position is more nuanced than she makes out but I do not want to get sidetracked into an argument with her. I stop complaining that Ross is never at home and tell her about the corporate hoes flyer. We are as one on that topic.

Liz can be quite scary but at least she is intelligent. For years she had a long-term boyfriend, Jeff, whom she grumbled about consistently, then – out of the blue, or, more precisely, out of the department of Law and Criminology at Aberystwyth University – came Libby. Libby has many sterling qualities. She is older than Liz and a wonderful cook; devoted to all things Welsh though she is not Welsh herself. She cooked roast rump of black-faced lamb for my parents when they visited while on holiday in Cardiganshire. I felt she'd known him personally, my mother said. His farm, his field, how he spent the summer.

Better prepared after the September fiasco, I use such bargaining power as I have to stop Ross from absenting himself on school nights. However, for five consecutive weekends he sleeps away. He is at Jude's house. He has told me a million times. He sets off and returns on his bike; he is a bike ride's distance from home. Why would he cycle fifty miles on a wet Friday evening? His bike is crap. He has never known anyone with a crappier bike. It will conk out. He can't be 'anywhere'. 'Anywhere' is ninety-nine point nine, nine, nine per cent unfeasible as a destination. He isn't shouting at me. If he is I deserve it. I drive him nuts. Anyway, why do I need to know?

The arguments always boil down to that. 'Why do you need to know?'

Jude's surname gives some clue as to his parentage. His mother is Bennet and his father is Dutch. They live in Crews Hill; a place that in the most far-reaching of the *London A to Zs* – the *Master Atlas of Greater London* – is surrounded by white patches. There is a grown-up sister, or maybe she is a half-sister, who lives in Barcelona. Dirk Neerhoff is an eye doctor, Teresa Bennet is an eye doctor. What, both eye doctors?

That last question does for me. The handle comes off the spade. No more digging. I am left with my own impressions. A fifties house; the kind with a chain-link fence and a frosted-glass bathroom window on the first floor, visible from the road. Grass verges to the pavements. A golf course or two at the back. No bus service – or maybe one of those small single-deckers that potter from nowhere to nowhere bearing an alpha-numeric sign. As for the Bennet-Neerhoffs themselves, I imagine a blond square-headed man and a Roman Catholic English woman. I envisage a darkened room, in the centre of which stand a slit-lamp machine and a white-coated person peering in, seeing everything, noting everything, while the patient views a tiny tunnelled world through a haze of yellow fluorescein.

Strangely, although I construct a view of the Bennet-Neerhoff set-up that in a dreamlike way veers between the numinous and the diabolic and contains some precise images, I form no picture of Jude. He is the empty space in the frame.

I tell Ross that it is wrong to accept hospitality indefinitely without returning it. Reciprocity, it is called. Someone gives you something and you give something back. Ross says he knows what reciprocity means. Invite Jude here for a change. Silence. Well, make it happen.

9

I finally get hold of a telephone number for Jude's family from Ginny Lu at the end of October. It is a mobile number and I have no idea whether I will get through to Dr Bennet or Dr Neerhoff. Ginny does not know whose number she has been given. She is friendly and brisk.

The advantage of the telephone when introducing myself to someone new is that appearance is irrelevant. All the same, I glance in the mirror that hangs over the fireplace in the front room before calling the Bennet-Neerhoff number. I have no idea whether this is a good time. Sevenish on a Friday evening. I do not want to interrupt a clinic or their supper.

My hair, due for a cut, falls in dense, uneven clusters to my shoulders and resembles the outline of a larch tree. This dishevelment really is of no consequence though it can affect my mood. What I look for are signs that I am 'together', as people used to say. I look calm enough so I move away from the mirror, press the numbers and lift the phone to my ear.

'Hello.' It is a thin little voice against a hiss that grows louder.

'Hello. Teresa? I'm Lorna, Ross's mum. I hope this isn't a—'

The signal cuts out.

Dr Bennet might have been driving, or dealing with a gas leak, so I do not try again immediately. I feel relieved to have made contact, however brief. I now know there is someone I can speak to – the mother, not the father – and that Teresa sounds more like a child than the efficient, imperious person I feared. She exists. That takes a weight off my mind. Ginny Lu is the parents' rep for Ross's year group and everything within her scope is bona fide.

I pour myself a glass of wine and put a wash on.

At around nine o'clock, I call Teresa Bennet again. She seems somewhat distracted – but pleasant.

'Ross? I haven't seen him yet but he's probably here somewhere,' she says. 'Do you want me to find him?'

A dog is barking in the background. Her voice is reedy more than girlish and she is called Frances. I apologise for getting her name wrong and say how kind she is to put up with Ross and that we would love to reciprocate and have Jude to stay.

'Oh, yes,' Frances says. 'Nice idea. Sorry, the dog's going a bit mental. I'll have to go and feed her.'

41

Frances Bennet does not sound like an eye doctor, not an eminent one, anyway. I am also surprised to hear about the dog because toxoplasmosis is a terrible eye disease that children, born and unborn, can get from uncooked meat and the faeces of pets. I worried enough about it myself when the boys were little and was forever checking their hands and telling them to watch out for dog turds when they beat paths through the long grass, flailing seed heads as they went.

10

I tramp through Grovelands Park for what will be the last time this year. For a short while I am on the wing – airborne. I shall miss the path over undulating ground, the stream that runs invisible among the trees crossed by little wooden bridges, the sound of children's voices in the wood. The ground is firm, not yet spongy or fungal, and the grass smells fresh. The clocks go back at midnight. From then on the gates will shut at 16.45 and progressively earlier times. It seems too soon to call off daylight saving while there are good ways to spend it. I have lost the sense that autumn is a beginning. School and university drive it into you and growing older drives it out. Until April, I shall be walking between Palmers Green and Winchmore Hill along suburban pavements.

Saturday tea at my father's flat in The Heronry. The weekly pattern repeats. I cry off if something crops up and William accepts any change with equanimity. Quite simply, I like to see him and my occasional feelings of being trapped in an arrangement that could go on indefinitely are checked by remembering my mother's death from cardiac arrest – the suddenness of it. Nothing goes on indefinitely.

The park has altered little in the last hundred years. Humphry Repton laid out its beautiful bones. The civic amenities were added early in the twentieth century. I can imagine myself here as a child, or my parents or grandparents, also as children, because as types in a landscape we are cut and come again. The big house, built in the 1790s by John Nash for a Tottenham brandy merchant, was never demolished and has passed through many changes of use, mostly medical; it has been a military hospital, a convalescent home and, more recently, a private clinic where in 1998 General Pinochet was held under house arrest. He must from time to time have looked out of a window, contemplating the English park – a gift to the public made by Southgate Urban District Council in 1911 – though he probably would not have stood for long, as he had undergone a back operation. His gaze left no visible mark. The pitch and putt, the bowling club, the single table with umbrella in front of the shack selling ice cream and drinks exist on their own terms. The clinic lays no claims to the park. The only medical reference is on the 'Lost' notices pinned to two trees; one near the Palmers Green entrance gate, the other on the Winchmore Hill side. They have been there since the summer holidays and are now faded and rain-battered.

Each displays a photograph of a tabby cat with three white paws and the words, 'Gustav critically ill and needs his medication urgently'.

Ewan, Oliver and Ross would once have been passionately interested in the cat Gustav. They would have wanted to know where he had gone, what his illness was, how he had caught it, what his medication consisted of and whether he would be given it from a spoon. I used to like these conversations that went off in bizarre but predictable directions and were endlessly repeated. I tried to interest my little boys in General Pinochet but there was always something more Gustav-like that they would rather discuss. Dictators are all very well but what about the lost cat? It took me a while to adjust to infantile preoccupations but they became firmly fixed so that now, in middle age, they are intertwined with adult ways of thinking and I can waste time wondering who let go of a stray balloon and where it might come to rest.

In the dusk, the park becomes mysterious. Because it stands on a section of sloping valley that is not smoothly flat, it is impossible to take in the whole area at a glance. Pockets of land reveal themselves like photographic slides, subtly different from what came before, and people too can suddenly loom up. The evening dog walkers are a grumpy lot and sometimes menacing-looking. From an early age, Ewan was able to recite the names Dogo

Argentino, Fila Brasileiro, Japanese Tosa, Pit Bull Terrier, and claimed he could restrain any one of them with a magic muzzle. I avoid eye contact with a character whose two Staffies are straining on choke leads and, as he comes towards me, direct my attention to the lake that has just come into view. The sky is yellow – not the yellow of pollution but a clear, primrose colour that happens as the year turns towards winter – and is reflected in the water. Birds float, weightless as black silhouettes on the surface. A man sits on a bench staring at the lake, his face, in profile, lit by the setting sun. He wears a dark-coloured cagoule, with high-visibility stripes down the sleeves and across the back. They catch the light. A bicycle is propped beside him. Something about him is familiar but I cannot place him. Then he moves. He searches in a pocket for his phone, half-rises from the bench, and I recognise the long neck and ungainly movements of Alan Child, Ross's English teacher.

An early firework goes off; a sudden flare, a bang. I hurry by with my head down.

11

'Why did you tell me Jude's mum was called Teresa? Her name's Frances,' I say to Ross, who has reappeared in my absence. He is perching on the boxes stacked in the hall and is eating baked beans from a tin with a spoon.

'Yeah, I know,' Ross says.

'Then why did you say she was Teresa?'

'I didn't.'

'You did. I distinctly remember Teresa. Teresa and Dirk. I thought she might be Roman Catholic.'

'What's your problem?'

'None. I don't have a problem. She might have been named after the saint. Actually there were two of them. Two St Teresas.'

'I've only ever heard of Francis. St Francis of Assisi? Didn't he talk to birds, or something?'

I stare at him. 'That's a totally different name. It doesn't sound the same. I'd never have muddled them up.'

'You're nuts, Mum.'

I am convinced he is wrong. I did not misremember or mishear. Working with registers and documents, I know my Smiths from my Smythes. Ross is quite capable of saying names at random to keep me quiet. Maybe Dirk is not right either, though that would be unusually inventive on Ross's part.

'Is it Dirk?' I ask.

'Is what dirk?'

He is halfway up the stairs by then so I leave it. I wish I had not started on the topic. I should have asked about the dog. He is probably fond of the dog after all this time. I imagine Ross and Jude running over fields. Crews Hill is far enough out of London for fields. The boys sit with their backs to a hedge and smoke dope and the dog, in the open air, escapes intoxication. I want to know more about Frances – what she looks like. But none of the boys answers that kind of question. Randal, though he possesses some visual sense, tends to say 'Normal' or 'Short'. My father is not much use. Only my mother went in for detail.

12

An hour later, the doorbell rings. I switch on the hall light and walk along the passage. I open the door. A girl stands on the step.

'Hello,' I say.

'Hello.' The girl hangs back. 'Is Ross in? He said to come round.'

'Hi. Yes, he is. Come on in.'

The girl comes forward and onto the mat. Her head is down. When she looks up I see first a heart-shaped hairline, then her face. The girl wipes her feet. She is wearing heavy lace-up boots, jeans, a dark coat with a hood and a bulky woollen scarf that is wound several times round her neck.

'I'm Lorna, his mum.'

The girl nods.

'Ross's room is off the half landing. Follow the music.' I notice the discarded baked-bean tin and pick it up. The spoon rattles inside like coins in a charity collection box. I hold the tin, smiling foolishly as the girl strides up the stairs two steps at a time, with her outdoor clothes on. The house sighs and sags.

When the food is ready I go into the hall and call. Above my head, the bass beat continues. I eat. Every now and then, footsteps thud across the floor. In a small house there is no privacy and yet in any one room, behind a closed door, anything could be happening. It is like the workings of the brain. The family living area is the prefrontal cortex and the rooms upstairs are the amygdala where neurons growl and rattle their chains. On the worktop, the food cools. I help myself to crispy bits of chicken skin.

Ross slopes into the kitchen soon after half-past eight, the girl behind him.

'There's chicken. Three-quarters of a bird. Some roast veg. Probably a bit cold by now but you can stick it in the microwave. Help yourselves. Guess who I saw in Grovelands Park coming back from Grandad's?' I say.

Ross ignores my question and begins to rummage in the fridge.

'Mr Child,' I say. 'He was sitting by the lake, looking soulful. Ross, can you get your head out of there. What are you looking for?'

'Something to eat.'

I explain again and in more detail what the options are.

'What did you do with my prawn balls?'

'Threw them out.'

'You can't do that. They were mine. There were two left.'

'You should have eaten them last week. They don't keep.'

'But I've only just remembered them.'

'Tough.' I turn to the girl. 'Sorry about the trivial level of conversation in this house.'

'No worries,' the girl says.

'I'm going to make toast, Jude. Brown or white?' Ross says.

'You're Jude?' I say on a rising inflection.

'Ye-es,' she says cautiously and glances at Ross for reassurance. 'Who did your mum think I was?'

Her hair is as dark as pickled walnuts and she wears it part-shoved behind her ears. Her eyes turn down at the corners like teardrops on their sides. She is the same height as Ross; sturdy, in a lean way. In a howling gale, she will stand firm. She bears no resemblance to the parents of my imagination.

'Sometimes I'm a bit dim. You live in Crews Hill, don't you, Jude? Tell me about it. I've never been there.'

Ross squirms. 'We've come to get food. Don't make conversation.'

'I'm casting my mind back in the hope of finding lost pronouns that will prove you deliberately led me astray over Jude's gender.'

51

'What do you want to know about Crews Hill?' The girl does not return my smile.

'Anything. What are the high points?'

'It's normal.'

Jude squeezes into the gap between the table and the sink unit and sits down opposite me.

'Ross, the toast.'

'I know, Mum.' Ross is chiselling lumps out of the chicken with an ordinary knife.

'It's smoking.'

'OK.'

'Use the skewer. Would you like something to drink, Jude? Juice? Water?'

'Stop saying her name. It's really irritating me.'

'Coffee, please. Cappuccino.'

'I'll get it,' Ross says. 'You don't have to hang around.' He means me.

'Doigy, did you paint that cow?' Jude points to a picture sellotaped to the back of the dresser.

'No,' Ross says. 'Actually, it's an auroch. Ewan did it when he was four, allegedly.'

'It's good,' Jude says. 'I like children's art.'

I stand up. 'Right. Shout if you need anything.'

I go through the doorway and along the passage. Ross and Jude keep silent as I ascend the stairs. They communicate wordlessly because there is no door to the kitchen. I wonder how they will achieve froth. The Bennet-Neerhoff kitchen, I assume, has a fancy coffee-making machine. I stand in front of the door to the loft room and remember the egg whisk, an old wire thing with a green handle. I stop myself from running back down to rummage through the drawers.

I knock gently and push the door. I peer in. Ewan is on the bed, turned on his side, under the duvet. I sense something provisional about his posture, as if he suddenly flung himself down and, as if to confirm this, he shifts. His right foot emerges, covered by a sock and edged by the leg of his jeans.

Sometimes there is an odd atmosphere around Ewan. It is like wobbling air above a hot engine; the light bent by patterns of air pockets at varying temperatures. Nothing relating to him seems quite stable, though his life, as far as I can read it, is one of utter monotony.

13

Cautiously, I feel under the front seat of the car, prodding between parts of the metal undercarriage that are sticky to the touch. Stones and grit. Hardened mud. Coins. Receipts and parking tickets. Rain drums on the roof. It is dark down here in the footwell, like the entrance to a coal chute. The ribbed rubber mat that protects the carpet is clogged with gravel, possibly from the drive of the Bennet-Neerhoffs' house. Gravel, once walked over, gets everywhere. I was hoping for a screwed-up ball of paper that once spread open would turn out to be the Performance Review 1 (PR1) appointments' sheet.

It is clearly important for parents to have an effective opportunity to monitor their son's or daughter's progress in their learning and development and for the students to be effectively supported from home in their studies and the whole thing strongly, clearly and effectively . . . http://www.LloydBarronAcademy. or/cobblingrubbishtogether/#sthash.p973000 Every-onetofulfiltheirpotential.

Perhaps Ross has it. One minute he was beside me, burdened by his physical presence as if it were a drag on his existence, or even a catastrophe, and the next –

I often marvel at the way my wholly material sons vanish.

I get up from the mat and sit back in the driver's seat. The school buildings are reflected in a surface sheen of water. Every window on every floor is bright with class-room lights. More cars arrive and swoosh to a stop in the marked bays of the car park. Two boys emerge through the sliding door of a camper van. Harry and Gervase Lupton who at the age of eleven were as alike as piglets but now distinguish themselves with hair gelled into differential peaks. I still can't tell them apart, though apparently it is easy and I must have defective eyesight because no one else talks about the twin thing anymore and I am stuck in some time-warp. I pick fragments of dirt from my nails.

When the downpour eases I lock the car and make my way along the line of 4x4 vehicles that have recently arrived and still give off engine heat. I cross the fore-court, dodging immense puddles. Two women are standing on the front steps of the main building, hoods up. They seem to be waiting as well as talking. As I approach, one of them raises her hand in a salute and I recognise Deborah Lupton, and the non-waving Ginny

Lu, and realise that they are waiting for me. Even a brief conversation with these foolproof parents can make me feel as weak as an invalid. Exposed on the tarmac with nowhere to hide, I gesticulate, tap at my head, mime that I have left something in the car. I make signs that they should go on in. Deborah and Ginny love school life. They plunged into the mini-world of constraints, clatterings and smells, glad of a second immersion. They want something. Money or time for sponsored swims, the Christmas Charity Fayre, a sixth-form ski trip, a day trip to Belgium. As I retrace my steps between parked cars to complete the pathetic charade, I catch sight of a woman and her daughter staring at me through a windscreen. I repeat my little routine, though with less bravura, and smile weakly at their astonished faces.

'Ross not with you?' Mr Milner licks his thumb and shuffles through a pile of papers.

'He *was* here. I drove him here. I've sent texts and left messages but . . .' My sentence tails off. 'I see the silent film is on again. It's beautiful. I think I caught sight of Oliver, this time. They're just children, aren't they? Without a soundtrack of their voices they seem in some way doomed.'

Douglas Milner crosses his legs. His trousers fold into

a kind of pouch at the crotch. He wears a purple shirt and a non-matching purple tie. Our chairs face each other. A third and fourth empty chair stand on either side. Underneath one of them is a small pool where someone placed a sopping umbrella.

'Do you have your PR1 appointment schedule there?' He bypasses the dreamy small talk.

'No. I'm doing this from memory.'

The suspended foot in a chunky shoe is an independent form of life. Two creases above the metatarsal bones are like the frown on the brow of a dog.

'Ah well, never mind. Let's bring up the grid.' Mr Milner summons up Ross's maths marks on his tablet and begins to go through them. The content is familiar, the list of nit-picking complaints, reprised in a genial manner.

'Good evening, Ms Parry.' A woman creeps up on me. 'I'm Mary de Silva, head of RE, doubling up as events manager. I have your email about Year 12 work experience, thank you very much. Hang on, let's just find it. Oh, here it is. "Unfortunately, I work with members of the public who are not DBS checked. I am unable to offer work placement." Yes, that's all absolutely fine but what I'm thinking is there's no reason at all why you shouldn't be one of our notable speakers this term. We don't have an archivist on the list and it would be a wonderful opportunity for the students to hear about . . .' Mary de Silva rattles through her pitch. Her head bobs as she scrolls down the screen. She is wearing a strange garment – a shrug, is it called? – made of red lace, over a drab, rather masculine dress.

'Yes, you're so right about members of the public. Just the other day . . . No, I won't go into that. I'm afraid I'm going to have to disappoint you over the speaking. It would simply be misleading for me to come and talk. There are no jobs in archiving.'

'That shouldn't be a problem. I have the schedule here. I'll run the dates past you.'

I peel off my jumper and add it to the collection of clothes over my arm.

'It's incredibly hot in here, isn't it? No. I mean it. Libraries and archives are being closed. Any data that isn't packed off to China for recycling will be dense-packed into DNA and dance on a pinhead. It would be much more useful if you got hold of someone from HR at Pret a Manger.'

'I'll just run the dates past you,' Mary de Silva repeats. Her face takes on the complacent expression of an annoying soft toy.

As I approach Miss McKenna, Deborah Lupton cuts in front of me. 'We need to have a word with you, Lorna.

Have you seen Mr Child? Where is the wretched man? Don't run away without speaking to me.' She takes off the hiker's backpack she is wearing, plonks herself down in front of Miss McKenna and gestures at the chairs to her right and left. Harry and Gervase obediently sit on them.

I move over towards one of the tilting windows. I push it open, but not so far that the rain comes in, and stand with my back to the breeze. Mr and Mrs Lu are smiling away with Mrs Anstey. Their daughter, Grace Lu, smiling. Mrs Lupton with the twins. The Levines. Hunter is six foot; taller than his father. Each family in its own little island, grouped around a teacher, shares noses and chins and smiles. In films and the theatre, all children look adopted. Hamlet never takes after Gertrude. Reality is more uncanny. The carpet squares are covered in the damp footprints of uncanny people. Ross is nowhere to be seen. Jude is also absent. A photo-portrait of Sir Graham Lloyd-Barron hangs above the microwave oven.

Over by the lockers, people wait to see the head. Tony Goode does not teach anybody. He shows people round, sponsors and local worthies, and once, in a fit of temper, pinned Danny Gage against the wall and raged against him which was a sackable offence but hushed up by senior management.

Whenever I come to this place, I feel as if I have never left. It all runs into one long evening. I send Ross another text. On the far side of the room Mr Frost guffaws.

14

On The Ridgeway, as we head in the direction of Crews Hill, the traffic slows.

'Could be an accident. We might be here for a while.' I glance in the wing mirror at an approaching police motorbike and then shift my gaze to the driver's mirror. 'How did you get on, Jude? Ross seems not to be a shining beacon of excellence.'

'I never saw anyone,' Jude says. 'When I heard that Mum wasn't coming I gave up.'

They are framed by the mirror's edge. Ross has his arm round her. He is wearing Jude's scarf and she is wearing his beanie. The black woolly hat is pulled down over her eyebrows.

'Did something happen? I'm sorry I didn't get to meet her.'

'We're tired, Mum. Can you please stop talking,' Ross says.

The motorbike speeds past the line of traffic, lights winking.

'I've no idea why you're tired. I did all the work *and* had to make excuses for you. It was extremely exhausting. Where were you all that time?'

'In the study space. Jude was too. We were reading *Hamlet*.'

'Admirable. I think I managed to speak to everyone – apart from Mr Child. Deborah Lupton was much exercised that he hadn't shown up – though it doesn't take much to get Deborah excited. Was he also in the study space? Perhaps taking the part of Voltemand. "I have found the very cause of Hamlet's lunacy."'

'Hang on – Doigy, move your hand. Look at this, Lorna.' Jude passes her phone to me through the gap between the front seats. My sons never let me near their phones. They are pirate chests marked 'secret'.

I glance at the screen. A figure in a doorway. The shot is from behind.

'Who are we looking at?'

'Mr Child. Don't you recognise him?'

'He seems to be wearing a small rucksack. We're moving again. I must concentrate on the road, Jude.'

'He went into this cupboard place on the first floor of Old School yesterday lunch-time. He was carrying a chair. I don't know how long he stayed there. Mr Frost came past and I had to go.'

'Furtive behaviour,' I say. 'What's in the cupboard?'

'I'll find out. What do you think he was doing?'

'Maybe mindfulness training. He sits and meditates?'

'Weird place to choose.'

'Hmm,' I say. 'The lure of tight spaces. Where I work, a man – Chris Orrick – was doing some research into a wartime civilian disaster at Bethnal Green Tube station. March 1943. Hundreds of people poured down the stairs in terror at what they thought was a bomb but turned out to be a British anti-aircraft rocket fired from Victoria Park. A woman tripped and everyone fell on top of each other. The government played the incident down and failed to give a proper account.'

'What's she on about?' Ross says.

One hostile. The other friendly.

'Someone called Yorick. Aren't you listening?'

'So what's new?' I continue. 'Something similar happened at the Hillsborough Stadium in 1989. Do the powers that be learn from previous botched cover-ups? No, they do not. Covering up is one of their specialities. Together with, we now learn, widespread surveillance. Why am I talking about this? Oh yes, Chris Orrick appeared to be unnaturally interested in the *crush* aspect of the episode.' I give a brief impersonation of Mr Orrick's self-strangulation – mostly sound effects, since I have to steer the car. 'I fear it may be a fetish,' I say.

I am aware of hushed fumbling sounds of cloth brushing

cloth. The retirement project of a stranger. There is no reason why they should be interested.

The intervals between street lamps become further apart. Each lamp is circled in white mist. I have no idea where I am going.

'Jude. You're going to have to direct me.'

A pause for disengagement. 'Oh, are we at the round-about? Thank you for driving me home. It's really out of your way. I didn't know we'd get stuck.'

'I'm glad to do it.'

Jude gives me instructions for the last half-mile. We arrive at a lane that goes nowhere and hers is the last cottage in the row. I see a sign to a riding school. Beyond are dark fields.

I stare ahead through the purposeful silence of a kiss. Jude says goodbye and gets out of the car. Cold air rushes in. I wait with the engine running while she walks up the front path. She puts her key in the lock. As Jude opens the door, I hear barking and see a dog rush towards her. It slithers at the last moment across a black-and-white tiled floor.

15

The kitchen smells strongly of bleach and seafood, like a fish market at the end of the day. I am making more effort with the cleaning, and trying out new recipes. I put random ingredients into the search bar and the Internet concocts something more or less edible. Pistachio-crust salmon with spaghetti. It is dead simple. If you don't have any Thai fish sauce, it says, just use Worcestershire which is fine by me.

When I look at Jude, with her unmade-up face and downward-turning eyes, I want to throw away the demeaning aspects of adulthood. Ugly clothes, shoes, bags, stub ends of make-up, rancid perfumes. She has a spectacular effect on Ross. It is like the weather clearing once a front has moved on. His smile follows her around the room. She communicates in gusts and wears Ross's skull-print sweatshirt. They have bought matching ear cuffs.

'What's this?' Ross asks.

'Salmon.'

'Stick to the pasta, Jude. I'll put some ketchup on and

we'll take it upstairs.' Ross holds out two plates. He gives her a surreptitious grin. His Spider-Man sleeping bag is rolled out on the floor above us. For my sake, I suppose; or for his, on my behalf. It is Friday evening and Jude is with us again for the weekend. Without any explanation, Ross has stopped going to Crews Hill.

'No, you won't,' I say, as I dole out the portions. 'You eat down here.'

I tip the fish onto the dishes in such a way that the crust is underneath. The nutty bit looks like greeny particles of burnt mould I am trying to hide.

'Why?' Ross says.

'House rule.'

'With exceptions,' he says, a hint of bitterness in his voice.

'If you're at home at twenty-one, I'll reconsider.'

'No way. No way will I be at home then.'

'We'll eat in the kitchen, Doigy. It's OK. Sit down.' Jude is already at the table. She breaks up the fish and distributes flakes into the pasta with artistic precision. She tucks her hair behind her ears to eat. Her skin is as smooth as new soap.

'I'm afraid my presentation skills lack finesse,' I say.

'Don't worry about it.' Jude pauses. 'Doesn't Ross's brother ever eat with you?'

'Ewan? Very seldom,' I say.

'Does he leave his room?'

'Oh, yes.'

'The house?'

'Yes.'

'Where does he go?' Jude takes neat mouthfuls in between questions. She twirls the spaghetti and tucks in the loose ends with a flourish.

'Who knows? Along the streets, through Grovelands Park, Broomfield Park? I suppose he might get a train into town.'

'You give him money, then?'

'Yes. Not much.'

'Does he have a girlfriend?'

'Probably not. I don't know.'

'Has he ever had one?'

'I expect so.'

'They haven't come here?'

'No, Jude. But I don't know that I read much into that. Lola from nursery school used to come round to play. But since then there has been a dearth of—'

'What does he do all day long?'

'Draws, does stuff on the computer, goes out. I don't know exactly.'

'He should get a job.' She pronounces her consonants as if biting on them.

'Quite.'

'There are jobs if you're not too fussy. Baristas, shop assistants . . .'

I stand up, pick up my plate and tip what remains in the bin.

'Finesse,' Ross mutters. 'Fuck.'

16

I can't face speaking about Ewan. Has he thought of seeing a therapist / getting an internship / learning Mandarin or web design? The recommendations are eased into speech with kindness. I dread the 'What do your children do?' question. Other people seem to think I exist in a mental fog so soupy and thick that the simplest solutions have failed to occur to me. I expect it's a phase. They've been saying this for two years. It never occurs to them that the last person said it and the one before. 'Phase' is used in the sense of a period one's son passes through, never to return, though to me the word, commonly associated with the movement of the moon and the planets, defines a recurring thing. If Ewan's torpor turns out to be a recurring thing, some other woman can deal with it.

Ewan stays in his room for hours at a time. He watches television on his laptop and draws bizarre and beautiful illuminated letters; a calligraphy that is undermined by the use of biro. The content is fairly wide-ranging. 'A', for example, incorporates an arsehole as well as Aztecs and an arum lily. The basic colours of blue, black and red intertwine on a jotter pad and produce, from a distance, the effect of a fantasy map or engraving. He comes down to the kitchen for food and to make tea or coffee, mostly in my absence. Sometimes he exchanges a few words with me or his brothers if he meets us on the landing; at others he slips past; a tall, sad-faced youth with hunched shoulders. Once or twice a week, I am aware that he leaves the house. I hear the front door click shut and later the key in the lock as he lets himself in. He goes straight upstairs. He can be away for as little as twenty minutes, or as long as four or five hours.

He is usually dressed in the daytime: jeans, sweatshirts, jumpers – normal clothes, though they hang off him. He keeps his hair washed and must from time to time have it cut because it never grows longer than collar length. He is lanky, hollowed out under his ribs, but I know he eats. He takes food up to his room. Used plates and bowls end up on the floor. It is squalid to leave them there but they come back down in the end. I am not a chambermaid. He has the run of the house and I like to think that he makes use of the extra space when I am at work; that he sits in the kitchen, or the living room, watches television, spreads himself about a bit. I have no idea what he does. He completed two terms of a BA Hons degree in Film and Literature. He has no job. He makes no contribution to the household or to society.

I look at his face. I am so used to it that I do not know what to make of it. I saw it at the beginning. If I had to recreate it I would use clay rather than wood because its changes are subtle. I would have to feel them under my fingers. He becomes watchful, distracted, alert, forgetful with a gradual dawning, and often I quake seeing the look on his face.

At least he goes out, I said to Randal, soon after Ewan abandoned his degree course. That has to be a good sign. He has fresh air and takes some exercise. He wears trainers and appears fit. We don't need to know what he's doing; he is an adult. Let's assume he meets up with friends, I said. I hope that's right, Randal said, though he was usually the positive one. Well, why not? I said. He has his phone, he can fix things up. I hope that's right, Randal said. Please stop saying that, I said. It rattles me. I understood what Randal implied. I had looked up the classic signs of depression, though I already knew what they were; a slippery list that applies to most people some of the time. The experts seem to agree that in the tick-box five is the key number, the same that they recommend for daily consumption of fruit and vegetables.

17

'Hello. Only me,' I call out.

I am holding the keys that I use to let myself into William's flat. The living-room door is ajar.

'This is Jane Brims,' my father says as I enter. 'She's one of Helena's cousins. She was passing by and called in to see me.'

Jane Brims acknowledges me with a dull smile. She is tucked into the corner of the sofa, holding a tumbler that rattles with ice. Old ice it must be, frozen into cubes many years ago. My mother had cold-sensitive teeth and William, my father, dislikes his gin and French diluted.

'Help yourself to a drink, Lorna,' he says. 'There's a bottle of red open in the kitchen.'

'No, thanks.'

He looks at his watch. 'It's coming up to five o'clock. I thought we might stretch a point.' He turns to the woman. 'Lorna drops by to see if I'm all in one piece. Generally, I am.'

Jane Brims crosses her legs. She is wearing tapered

black trousers, floral-patterned socks and red pumps. She takes a sip from the glass.

'Aren't I, Lorna?' my father says.

He is sitting in the hoop-backed chair that my mother, Helena, reupholstered. It faces the three floor-to-ceiling windows that take up one whole side of the room and let in the sky. There is little wall space for furniture and bookshelves. Even after the great cull that took place when William left the old house, what remains is packed in tightly and the arrangement, though artful, is not a complete success. A stranger, walking in, would guess correctly: elderly person or persons in a contemporary apartment.

'Sorry, Dad?'

'Generally in one piece?'

'Yes. Yes, you are.' I am usually more encouraging – and would add that he is doing really well, or some such phrase – but I am inhibited by the presence of the woman on the sofa.

'You're hovering,' my father says. 'Sit down. Or are you rushing off immediately? Quite often she's rushing off.' He speaks in a kindly voice without resentment.

I drop the keys into my bag and sit on the arm of his chair, surprised, as I always am when I first arrive, by being at a standstill. Once I cross the threshold and perch myself, the day that has moved along stops.

Jane Brims is a full ten years younger than William, possibly more; a striking woman with a serviceable layer of flesh – the equivalent of a couple of thermal vests – evenly distributed over her person, and this conserves her youth. Her unlined face is long and large; her eyes, brown as a dog's, remain soulful even when her mouth – the business end of her face – tightens in annoyance. She sits firmly on the sofa, in an upright posture, more interviewer than interviewee, without a shred of diffidence. The legs, more skittishly arranged, stretched out and crossed at the ankles, reveal the floral socks. Are we supposed to admire them?

She has been on a classical tour of Tunisia and visited the ancient Roman city of Dougga and the remains of the city of Carthage. There was an optional camel ride.

William starts to tell his piano-recital story from the never-to-be-repeated cultural cruise on the Danube. Jane sits tight-lipped through his plodding account and the second it comes to an end launches into a morning at the troglodyte cave dwellings of Matmata, beginning with the early start and breakfast on the minibus.

She speaks of white walls and blue-painted doors and progresses to Lars Homestead, the residence of Luke Skywalker, Aunt Beru Lars and Uncle Owen Lars. My father, who knows nothing of *Star Wars*, is taken aback by the mention of these Norwegian-sounding relatives and asks tetchily, 'Which holiday are you on now?'

In the lulls, I focus on the views north-west, over suburban crescents and closes, towards the turreted buildings of Highlands, the former Northern Convalescent Fever Hospital, now converted into apartment blocks. The windows of William's apartment resemble unrolled Chinese scrolls. The balcony rail appears as a consistent dividing line in each and the vistas of lighted buildings and bare-branched trees occupy successive sections of the panorama, with their own clouds or cloud parts, pale against the sky. At the end of November, the sun has set by four-thirty.

She starts as she means to go on, I think, though quite why the phrase jumps into my mind, I don't know. I have no idea who Jane Brims is or why she is ensconced in William's living room, looking like part of the furniture. My father's reference to Jane passing by – where? The Heronry, Winchmore Hill? – seems inadequate and even disingenuous; a sleight of hand that I find disconcerting. I am not inclined to ask questions. Is she a Yates or a Finch? Suffolk or Middlesex? Probing will prolong the visit and validate the woman's presence. Jane Brims might question me in return – though she has shown no interest in me thus far – and then I would have to elaborate on my sons' ages and education, my work, where we live;

the usual rigmarole. I prefer to sit gormlessly on the arm of my father's chair.

I have got into the habit, before I leave, of asking if there is anything William wants. This triggers anxious thoughts in him. It generally turns out that he has lost some household item – the kitchen scissors or the window key – or he wants me to read a letter from the managing agents of the flats.

William hesitates, then, 'No, nothing to report. All's well,' he says.

One thing my mother did that I failed to appreciate while she was alive was to make it possible to communicate with my father. She was both interpreter and maître d'. She was the oil that allowed a frictionless flow. I wish I had a recording to remind me how it was done. Even without Jane Brims on the scene, talk with William can be stilted and a little bit sticky though we are full of goodwill towards one another. I have hopes that as we get used to the new situation we will find it easier. My mother, rather than an absence, will preside over us again or maybe we will just rub along without her.

18

The grilles are down over the entrance to St James's Park station. We all stream back the way the way we came, past the free-newspaper stand, past doorway sleepers and unoccupied rolls of bedding, past the *Big Issue* seller, in his Santa hat, and the two lumbering, human-sized furry animals who beseech with their paws and hold out buckets for cash. Spangly light from the shops is reflected in puddles.

'Does this mean Victoria station's shut too?' a woman asks.

The pedestrian signal by The Albert turns from green to red and back to green but the crowd of office workers and shoppers underneath a canopy of bobbing umbrellas has to wait behind the outstretched arms of a police-woman until she gives permission to go. Buses labour, stopping and starting, the passengers masked by a blur of condensation. Wheels splash in slow motion.

'How much longer?' someone calls out.

'It's always the same,' the woman says, confidingly. 'They favour the traffic. If we're on foot, we don't exist.'

My phone rings. I have trouble disentangling it from my coat pocket. Drips land on my face as the umbrella tips sideways. I press the phone to my ear. Through the sound of juddering engines, I hear the word 'duck'. Doug? Dirk. Got it.

'Oh, hello, Dirk,' I say. 'There's a lot of background noise. I'm sorry.'

'You are at the airport check-in?'

'No. I've just left work. Hang on a sec. We're being allowed across the road.'

In the crush of pedestrians surging forward, I manage to hang onto the phone. The woman who spoke to me jams her open umbrella against mine. We are trapped in a moving, makeshift tent as the rain beats down on us.

'I have been meaning to thank you for having Jude to stay,' Dirk says. 'It has been frequent.'

'Not at all. We love to see her.'

'I hope she's no trouble.'

'No, she's no trouble at all. It's a pleasure to have her in the house.' We reach the other side and I walk briskly into the external lobby of the House of Fraser, formerly the Army and Navy Stores. I contrive, one-handed, to put down the umbrella. The woman has vanished, though momentarily I thought she was with me for life.

'Is the weekend of the twenty-seventh to twenty-eighth of January also possible? Rather distant, I know, but I should like to make these dates secure. Normally they stay where they like without intervention from us parents. This is correct for their age group, isn't it? They are moving out of our clutches towards independence. On this occasion I am more formal because Frances and I will be away. If you need to kick her out we will not be there.' Dirk laughs. 'I'm only joking. Of course, we will keep our phones on.'

'Yes, that should be fine, Dirk.' I step to one side to allow a customer to pass. He pushes open the glass door into the store and a waft of warm, cosmetic-scented air escapes. I glimpse beauty gifts the size of timpani.

'We are going to Manchester. This is where we met. And the twenty-eighth of January is an anniversary, special to us. It will, I hope, be a worthwhile weekend. I think you have heard from Jude some of our difficulties. I won't bore you with them. They are, inevitably, quite boring if you yourself are not in the thick of them.'

I murmur something; nothing articulate, a sympathetic noise.

The doors open and again a cloying, synthetic floral smell meets the damp air. Two women come out, laden with shopping bags.

'She has talked a bit about you.' Dirk Neerhoff pauses. 'She gives me a flavour of your conversation.'

'Well, it's always lovely to chat with her. She's great.'

'She is quite a mimic!' Dirk Neerhoff gives a short, friendly laugh. 'I do not have this gift. The expressions too. She does the expressions.'

I glance at my reflection in the glass doors of the store. And then across the road, at the light beaming through the decorative etched windows of The Albert: the yellow brick pub, built in the 1860s, that is sandwiched between undistinguished office towers.

'Really?' I say.

'I feel we have met. I hope this will be a reality in the near future. The four of us? For coffee?' Dirk says.

'Good idea.'

'We will find a date. Unless a plan is made nothing happens. If we don't speak again before Christmas, have a very happy—'

I wonder whether the changed pattern of Jude coming to Dairyman's Road rather than Ross going to the Bennet-Neerhoffs is connected with whatever is happening at home. Perhaps the atmosphere is terrible. Perhaps her parents row all the time. Or weep. My pleasure at the turn of events – Palmers Green one, Crews Hill nil – seems, in some far-fetched sense, to be at the other family's expense.

19

It takes me two hours to get back to Palmers Green station. At the moment Deborah Lupton imposes herself, I am in a trance, ascending to street level in the mass of commuters returning from work. The stairwell is poorly lit; the steps intermittently padded by damp, discarded newspapers. Her voice penetrates my coat at the level of my thoracic spine and travels up to my ears. Through thuds of disordered footsteps, it reaches me. I am in a state of holding steady, semi-stoical and semi-absent like an animal, a horse or an ox, pulling a cart up a hill, urged on by an unseen driver. Trapped between bodies and a brick wall, the paint of which has flaked into map-like patterns of green and sand-coloured continents, I hold and shall continue to hold, as I do every day, until the press of moving, breathing people eases, and I am out in damp air, walking along Alderman's Hill, heading towards home and able to be human again. I keep my feet on the steps, all the while forced to feel the woman's breath on my neck and to hear the powerful broadcast that reaches me in gusts.

'. . . as you know, he failed to attend the performance review. Absolutely typical. What we have come to expect . . . didn't even have the nous to give a pathetic excuse . . . guess is, he knows he's floundering and didn't want to face the . . .' It is only through willpower and a reminder to myself of the social contract that I resist an overwhelming urge to give Deborah Lupton a backwards kick that will send her toppling down onto the upward-climbing strangers who will not know what has hit them.

Once on the level, I continue to press forward. I turn right out of the station but she grabs my sleeve.

I whirl round. 'Just stop it. Calm down. Your voice is so bloody loud, everyone can hear you.'

Her large, astonished face is close enough to be out of focus. The mouth twitches and opens. 'Well, I don't think anyone is—'

'They might be. You don't know that. We are not a million miles from school.' I blast words into the face and then take a step back.

Deborah is staring at me as though I were a family comedy that had flashed up a scene of indecent assault. 'Point taken, Lorna.' She stands firm in her waterproof trousers. Her wellington boots are a foot or more apart.

'Say what you've got to say.' I breathe in and I breathe out again and by the second breath I see my surroundings. We are in front of the pharmacy. The interior is lit but partly shielded from sight by notices. 'Do You Know your Cholesterol Levels?' 'Free Prescription Service'. A man smokes a cigarette in the doorway. The smell is oddly comforting. People walk past us. 'I'm sorry, Deborah. I lost my temper. I just need to get home.'

She wrinkles her nose and raises her upper lip; something between a sniff and a wary smile. 'All right, I won't mention his name but we know who we're talking about, don't we? I hope you're keeping notes, Lorna. I am. A, his setting and marking of coursework are haphazard. B, he aims at the lowest common denominator. C, he leaves lessons as soon as the hooter goes and never makes himself available to answer questions. D, he fails to enthuse. To sum up – an all-round lacklustre performance.'

She invites me round for a drink the following week to discuss an action plan. I agree to go though I loathe this kind of thing – middle-class people on their high horses.

'I scanned for viruses after he sent that email. I advise you do the same.'

'Which email are you talking about, Deborah? I haven't had anything.'

'It was blank. No content. No subject. But he sent it.

A.CHILD@lloyd-barronacademy.co.uk. Ginny Lu had one too. I haven't yet checked with the others. Ginny says he may be *depressed*.'

'Perhaps he is.'

I knock on Ross's door to report on the conversation with Dirk. All family information should be in the open.

'What will you say to them?' Ross asks, referring to the coffee plan.

I say that I guess we will just chat.

'Why? You don't know them,' he says.

'I realise I don't but it's good to be friendly to people. These difficulties Dirk mentioned, have you any idea . . .?'

'They'll get a shock when they see you,' Ross says.

'Why?'

'I don't know why. But they will.'

'Tell Jude her dad called, will you,' I say.

'Meaning what?'

'Not meaning anything. It's polite to tell her.'

He slaps the side of his head. 'Man, you are bigging this thing up? This is disproportionate.'

I think, since the conversation is not going especially well, that I should ask him if he is up to date with his coursework. My mother used to tell me that this was a bad tactic and that it is better to wait for a pleasant spell before tackling an unwelcome topic. First, when is this pleasant spell? And second, why spoil it? I prefer to soldier on – unless we are eating. I go in for any kind of appeasement at mealtimes.

20

CD Review follows the news on the car radio; different recordings of the same Schumann Trio meticulously compared, movement by movement. Scenery goes by, an irrelevant backdrop to the passages of music. I keep my eye on the road; on the stream of cars ahead and behind. Through the speakers, strings and piano rush forward in bursts of intensity against the pull of an opposing tide. It begins to drizzle so I switch the windscreen wipers on, then a squirt of detergent because the glass is greasy.

I am on my way to Brighton. Another year nearly over. Oliver with a new life, Ross with a new life, William widowed which is a kind of new life. The sump of the year. Memory and expectation defeated by shopping. A fir tree lies on the living-room floor under the bay window. I realised too late that it is not wedged into a block and will not stand upright. I have made online donations: £50 to Crisis, £50 to Shelter and £50 to www.arrest-blair.com and bought Jude a present. A scarf and a pair of sheepskin mittens. I wrapped them in shimmery paper and tied the ribbon in a big bow. The boys never spend Christmas at

Randal's. They are conservative about arrangements and act as a pack to thwart changes. There is an element of loyalty to me in their refusal but this is, I believe, subsidiary to their obstinacy. The first Christmas without Randal, I failed to put decorations up in the hall and living room and, as soon as the boys noticed, they questioned me belligerently. Randal had left at the beginning of the month: 6 December, the anniversary of the establishment of the Irish Free State. I get things astonishingly wrong. I try to adapt to my sons' increasing years and put away childish things, sometimes with a pang and sometimes with a light heart, but I had to unearth the large red honeycomb paper bell, the paper chains made from gummed strips on a long-ago Sunday afternoon, the strings of silver stars, from the cardboard box marked 'Brother' that had once contained a printer. I dusted them off, got the stepladder out from under the stairs and suspended the bell from the central light fitting, draped the paper chains from nails that my father had banged into the architrave for that purpose, twisted the strings of silver stars over the fireplace and around the banister rail. The boys stayed in their rooms while I performed the neglected rite and afterwards said not a word. I could tell from their faces that they harboured hurt feelings and thought, not for the first time, that the distance between making amends and getting something right from the outset is immeasurable and that it might well be better to brazen things out because brazening confers a feeling of strength whereas reparation debilitates.

Oliver has grown taller since October; he is also broader across the shoulders. He bears the invisible marks of a person who has got away and whose return will be temporary. He is a little more lordly than previously and a shade more polite. I remember a similar atmosphere of otherness around Ewan on his first vacation from university. The effect was stronger because he was the eldest and a pioneer. The burner was lit and the balloon lifting. Well, that's Ewan on his way, I thought.

Coming up to Pease Pottage, Oliver asks me to stop at the service station so that he can buy coffee. I dislike negotiating the interchange at Pease Pottage and feel sorry for anyone who lives there and has to grapple with it on a daily basis. From the A23 northbound, it is necessary to leave at J11, where the road becomes a motorway, turn right at the roundabout and immediately right again. I manage to do this in the correct order without being sucked onto the M23 or into the slipstream of a jumbo jet taking off at Gatwick airport. Aeroplanes fly low over the road there, stark and blackly three-dimensional against the sky – one-trick predators. I shall make thirty-six of these journeys. I totted them up. This is the fourth.

I have now covered the permutations: down with Oliver, back alone, down alone, back with Oliver. Each is subtly different and the one I like least is back alone.

For God's sake, Lorna, Randal said when I rang to let him know Oliver's dates. You don't need to ferry him about. I said, I don't ferry him about. I'm not that sort of mother. News to me, Randal said. Let him go on the train. Or by bus. Even better. The whole of humanity is at Victoria Coach Station. Let him learn. I did it for Ewan, I said. I can't not do it for Oliver. Exactly, he said. Look where it got him. Think.

Oliver returns with a lidded beaker and immediately the smell of coffee pervades the car. We set off again. After a few gulps, Oliver comes partly to life. He tells a funny story about a lab assistant and a flask of benzene and mentions the names of new friends. Following the burst of communication, he falls silent again. I tell him that Ross has a girlfriend, Jude.

'Ewan?'

'He's the same,' I say.

21

I am trying on a short, mainly green, tartan skirt in front of the bedroom mirror when my phone rings. The cupboard doors are open and garments strewn on the bed. My legs are bare and I am wearing old socks. I am practised enough to see beyond the immediate aesthetic disaster and make a judgement. Hideous. These sessions that might or might not fill a carrier bag for the charity shop prove what I do not quite believe, that we are a succession of selves rather than a single identity. I am not the woman who bought that skirt.

'I'm about five minutes away.' There is a whooshing sound of traffic in the background. It is Randal.

'Make it ten.' I gaze at myself in the mirror.

'Whatever are you up to, Lorna?'

'Nothing. I just need the extra minutes.'

There is a slight pause. 'Oh, OK then. I'll take the scenic route.'

Although the days and the times of Randal's visits vary, his appearances at Dairyman's Road are as much reiterations as my callings-in on my father at the Winchmore Hill flat. The randomness, over a given period, feels almost the same as a fixed routine. Randal presses his face to the glass of the front door – something he has always done. After dark his silhouette is light against black and in the afternoon, the reverse.

I call up to Ewan to tell him that his dad is on his way and send Ross a text. I take off the skirt and add it to the pile of clothes on the bed.

I put my jeans back on and attack my hair with a brush. It is now long enough to pull back into a stubby knot. I snap a band around the clump and fasten the loose ends with clips. Seconds later the doorbell rings.

'Hi, Lorna. Happy New Year.' Randal kisses me casually on the cheek; one side only. The chinstrap beard that was in evidence when he delivered the Christmas presents has gone.

I return the greeting and tell him that Ross is out with Jude and that I do not know when they will be home.

'Ewan?'

'In his room.'

'How is he?'

'Same.'

'I'll go on up then. See you shortly.'

Randal goes up the stairs two at a time and stumbles, as he generally does, at the point where the matting is loose. I hear him hammer on Ewan's door.

He is up there for about twenty minutes.

'Hmm,' he says when he reappears. He is a scientist and has his own thing going. He pretends to be less enmeshed in parental emotion. In any case, he no longer lives at Dairyman's Road.

He looks around the kitchen as if viewing it for the first time. The greasy cooker hood, a half-eaten banana on the table, Ewan's never-to-be-thrown-away painting of an auroch.

'What are you looking at?' I say.

'Sorry. Just making shapes.' He doesn't immediately comment on Ewan. Sometimes he doesn't.

'So, the girlfriend's still on the scene. Splendid. How old did you say she was?'

'Seventeen. Same as Ross.'

'You like her?'

'She's lovely. She's half Dutch, did I tell you that? Her parents are doctors. They've lived in different places. Leeds, Utrecht, London. Jude's well-travelled.'

'Where does she sleep?'

When he realises I am not going to reply Randal walks over to the back door and peers through the glass at the unmatching pieces of garden furniture, the barbecue fire pit without a grill rack, the collection of old bikes. The tree is the main feature. It stands tall and straight with its domed crown high above the suburban rooftops;

the bark cracked into jigsaw-puzzle shapes of light and shade. An earlier owner gave up the struggle to grow anything and paved over the entire plot. It is an expanse of moss-encrusted grey, partly hidden by fallen sycamore leaves. We had a long-term plan to break up the paving and redesign the space in a more pleasing way but years went by and we did nothing. I shall probably continue to do nothing.

22

Oliver and Ross faced their father's departure to North Hertfordshire in utter silence. The house that up to that point had been a single entity became a series of doors, floors, ceilings and stairs. They kept to their rooms in a more studied way and with greater secrecy, as if they were ghosts of past inhabitants, former lodgers who turned keys in the locks, undid their collar studs and loosened their braces. We were, in a sense, back to what we had once been. Mother with children at home. Two of them – and then three when Ewan returned from Warwick for the Christmas vacation. Although I went to work every day, I was the old retainer. There was a bleak simplicity to our life and, when the evenings and week-ends came, no sign of father. I worried for us all in our state of isolation. The thought that the atmosphere might have been different with daughters – or with another set of sons – brought no comfort. These were my sons and I could not change them.

My inclination to relax the rules was immediately thwarted. I had to put back the middle leaf that I had removed from the dining-room table and drag the sofa to its original position, facing the bay window. I was told not to play Shostakovich loudly, or Janis Joplin at all, and my suggestion that we might buy a pet was greeted with derision. It was as if they needed to experience our predicament in a pure state, unsoftened by adjustments. Home ritual that had previously hummed along in the background like an innocuous but essential item of domestic machinery exposed itself as the dark rhythm we dance to.

Here he is again, though, solid and faintly menacing in his new tight cord trousers.

'Let's go and sit in the other room,' I say.

We walk down the passage and into the living room. I carry the tea. Whereas in our married days I would have flopped down next to Randal on the sofa, now I take the armchair. He places his phone beside him.

'Unusual tea. What is it?' Randal sniffs at the mug.

'Holy basil with jasmine. "Take a sip of ancient Wisdom".'

'It's weird. Smells of turps.' Randal takes a gulp. 'He was on the phone when I went up.'

'On the phone?'

'Yes, walking about and talking. I admit he was under the duvet when I came in December but the boiler had packed up, hadn't it? I really don't think you were right, Lorna.'

I take a deep breath. 'Let's forget it, can we?'

'To be honest, it was one of the weirdest things I've ever heard anyone say.'

'It. Was. A. Joke.'

I have never learned not to expose mental speculation to Randal. He wants to establish facts when there are none and like a militant atheist, as long as there is a single believer left in the world he cannot leave the thing alone.

He rubs the lower half of his face and then picks up his phone and checks it for messages. One reason I find my father's company restful is that he fiddles only with unresponsive objects, his reading glasses or a biro, and although he might polish the glasses with his handkerchief, or make a note to himself with the biro, these items give him no feedback. I do not say that he gives me his full attention. He has never been flooded with fascination for me – I would be appalled if he changed in this respect – but no other presence intervenes. When we are together it is just him and me and a few everyday distractions.

Over the course of minutes in which I watch Randal and wait, I bottle up anger. Bottling up need not take years. It is equally effective in the short term.

'Are you losing interest, Randal?' I say in an offhand kind of way.

'Interest in what?' as he composes a reply.

'Ewan. There is still a problem. It hasn't been solved.'

He lays the phone down. 'Don't be ridiculous, Lorna.'

'I wondered whether he had become like a . . .' I pretend to search for a word. 'Calendar?'

Randal looks at me in bafflement. He has, I think, genuinely forgotten that in the self-justifying list of my failings that he used to explain his departure with Charmian he likened me to a calendar, a reminder of the passing of time. When he spoke the words, his face contorted with excuses, I imagined something more Pirelli. It was only as he continued with more mundane accusations that the women in swimwear faded and I saw instead my husband of twenty-odd years troubled by numbers – groups of thirty or thirty-one days – that ate away at his life. I had become too closely associated with the process: back to the wall, spiral bound. If only he had compared me to an hourglass.

The gate clicks.

'Here they are. Good.' Randal brightens.

I glance out of the front window. 'It's a boy putting a flyer though the door. Yes, there's the letterbox. Pizza delivery? What were we saying?'

'*Non lo so*. How's William?'

'He's doing well. I'll tell him you asked after him. I'm seeing him soon.'

'He'll be lost without Helena.'

97

'He manages.'

'Let me give you a lift to Winchmore Hill.'

'No. I like to walk. Thank you.'

At four o'clock Randal leaves.

I return to the living room and sit on the sofa. Through half-closed eyes I take stock of the scene in front of me – bay window, fireplace, mirror, books, pictures, armchair; its loose cover furrowed by recent occupation. I turn them into a kind of mosaic of colours and shadows in which no single object conveys a particular meaning – and wish I could do the same with my thoughts. I was once proud of my thinking. I graded and preferred: purple or black, Mum or Dad, Christmas or summer, slow change or revolution.

23

I went to the Luptons' house years ago. It is in one of the roads of tall Victorian terraced houses to the east of Green Lanes, the winding thoroughfare that runs from Mason's Corner at Winchmore Hill down to Newington Green and was once a drovers' route. The terraces fall away down the slope of the land, their gables a diminishing series of pinnacles. Ross, aged twelve, spent a weekend afternoon with Harry and Gervase. The Luptons kept a gong in the hall and at supper-time the family appeared in response to Deborah's rhythmical banging. Deborah's mother-in-law who lives in their basement staggered upstairs within a few minutes. She panted somewhat from the effort and from the long-term effect of smoking a thin cigar before dinner, a habit that Deborah forbade; indeed, she had made the renunciation a condition of Jean's moving into the house.

The Lupton set-up made quite an impression on me. I waited among cases of musical instruments, cricket equipment, a rubber dinghy, a coil of marine rope, a wheelchair, a hoist and a solid, square-shaped object with a pink padded top that I took to be a commode. A modest chandelier hung from the ceiling and the walls were covered with nautical charts. Deborah talked as she banged the gong, warning me of Jean who duly appeared, puffing and heaving herself up by the banister rail, in many respects a normal woman, though Deborah had made out that she was some kind of living corpse. When Jean had recovered her breath she chatted pleasantly with me. I could see that she was in no immediate need of the aids, apart from perhaps the wheelchair for longer outings, and wondered whether they were placed there as symbols of decrepitude to deter her from her smoking habit – rather like the vanitas in old art, the skull or the fallen petal. I detected a whiff of tobacco as she talked. Harry, Gervase and Ross tumbled down the stairs soon afterwards. 'It's you,' Ross said – a rare acknowledgement – and I caught a look of relief pass across his round face.

Deborah's plan to get a group of parents together in the run-up to Christmas failed. One by one, people cancelled and in the end only the Luptons and Simon Petridis, Evie's father, held onto the date. Emails passed to and fro as we tried to reschedule. Deborah said that it was like trying to herd cats. Work-related dinners, committee meetings, choir rehearsals, fiftieth birthday parties. They gave detailed explanations. I have less in the diary than the others though I have started seeing Richard Watson again in an on/off way and a Saturday morning meet-up with Dirk and Frances has been arranged. Oliver's term dates are pencilled in. The New Year at 10 Dairyman's Road is much like the old.

Deborah finally marshalled us and we settled on an evening in mid-January, two weeks into the term. As Giles Lupton hurries me through the hall and down into the basement, I have time to register that though the atmosphere of the house is the same as on my previous visit some of the paraphernalia has gone.

A fractured chorus of voices greets me. Hello, Lorna, Hi, Lorna, Hi there, as Giles shepherds me into the 'snug', the basement room on the garden side of the house. The parent-guests are already present: Cassie Styles, Ginny Lu and Deborah Lupton on a sagging sofa; Simon Petridis at a higher level on a dining-room chair; and Terence Levine, higher still, on a piano stool, though there is no piano in evidence.

The room is furnished in timeless English comfort style – pieces of old rug on the floor, baggy cushions, singed lampshades, a dying azalea in a pot, a cathode-ray tube television, a rusty bagatelle board propped against the wall – and smells of something from the first-aid box, TCP, or some similar antiseptic. The curtains are drawn. The one to the left is dark green velvet, sun-bleached on the inner edge; the one to the right, a bold print of stylised poppies, is smaller in every dimension and its hem falls short of the floor. I imagine some kind of accident involving paint or red wine, or an incident that ended with a tearing. A family member who ran amok or a desperate pet – a cat with exceptional climbing ability and rip-sharp claws, or a fabric-eating dog.

Giles pours a glass of wine for me. I find a spare chair and sit down. I recognise everyone. This is a conspiracy of the like-minded. Because of the email exchange, I now know their first names. No Bennet-Neerhoffs. In fact, no one new and no one who lives in social housing. Less than a third of Mr Child's English A-level group is represented.

'Let's cut to the chase, now we're all here,' Deborah declares.

'I'll just finish, if I may,' Simon Petridis says. 'Evie has to cover certain points in the assignments. "Assessment objectives" I believe they're called. But she doesn't know what they are. "That's ridiculous," I said to her. "Have you read Kafka? He is your ally, even though he's dead." If teachers are going to mark to some tick-box scheme – which I understand is current policy – they have to tell you what they expect from you. Otherwise, it's divination – mind reading. And what is in the mind of Alan Child?'

'Agreed. Third rate.' Giles Lupton takes out a hand-kerchief and polishes his spectacles.

Even without seeing the half-empty wine glasses, I can tell from their voices and faces that they experienced the

102

first rush of alcohol to the bloodstream a while ago. The time of the meeting – 18.45 – was as finely tuned as a doctor's appointment, and I am not late. As they hark back to earlier points of discussion, I consider this and, though I am aware that these people can work themselves into righteous indignation from a standing start in a matter of seconds, for the first ten minutes I scarcely hear what is being said. I try to work out if I missed a last-minute message or – a more paranoid interpretation – whether Deborah deliberately invited me to arrive later than the others.

'Do any of them meet the criteria?' Terence asks.

'I think maybe Grace has had a couple of high-band sixes,' Ginny says modestly.

Grace Lu is of a different substance from my boys. You could deposit her, say, in an audience at Wigmore Hall and she would look younger than everyone else by fifty years but not out of place. She would listen attentively and her phone would be off and hidden in her bag. I admire her hugely. And Ginny. I admire her too.

She recounts that, each week, Mr Child's English set leaves the sixth-form block and goes to the old school building for a lesson; something to do with timetabling. It is there that the worst of the Year 12 indiscipline breaks out. The students cram the desks together or sit on the wide sills and fiddle with the window ropes. They eat packed lunch. They talk among themselves.

'Maybe they're suffering from some kind of regression,' Simon says, his rolled r's like the purr of a cat. 'Returning to the old school, they revert to earlier behaviours.'

'Every Wednesday,' Giles Lupton says. 'Codswallop.'

'*Hamlet* and *Silas Marner*. Slit-your-throat time. Enough to make anyone gloomy. Please, Giles.' Cassie holds out her glass for a refill.

'He was a different person in his NQT year. It's as if all the spark's gone out of him.' Ginny alone of the group is drinking water and covers her tumbler with her hand as Giles does the rounds.

'"Suppose George Eliot hadn't told us that sixteen years have passed? Would we know? Are there any clues?"' Deborah's mockney accent causes a few smiles.

She occupies the central position on the sofa; not a commanding position, since she sits at its lowest point. With her feet planted flat on the ground and her body tilted forward, she gives the impression of being ready to rise. In wide combat trousers, topped with a double-breasted Aran cardigan, she occupies twice the space of her neighbours.

'It seems a fair question. I mean, by no means stupid,' Terence says. 'Or are you objecting to Mr Child's vowel sounds, Deborah?'

'Ah, but wait. "It's Chapter Sixteen," *your* bright spark said.' Deborah points a finger at me. '"Sixteen years. Numbers are a parallel universe."'

'George A. Elliott is a distinguished mathematician at the University of Toronto, famous for his work on operator algebras in Hibbert space. It is conceivable that—'

Giles flaps his hand at Simon, as if batting a fly away. 'Carry on, Debs. Say what you've got to say.'

'Ross went on for about ten minutes. Fairly tedious for the others.' Deborah shifts from side to side. 'Mr Child should have taken control of the situation. He should have said, "Well spotted but let's move on." Then little Cara started up. "I don't like it when books jump time. It's like you're told you've got a terminal illness. Say you're twenty and you're expecting to live another eighty years. Suddenly the doctor says you've only got two left."'

Cassie, who has been examining her fingernails, jerks up her head at the mention of her daughter and shoots Deborah a look of pure hatred. 'That was her step-brother,' she spits out. 'His last weeks were beyond terrible. A vet would have—'

'Ha, ha. All very amusing these anecdotes but let's progress, Debs.' Giles Lupton rocks on his heels, in front of the boarded-up fireplace. He waves an empty bottle. 'There isn't time for an adverse Stroop Effect. I don't know whether any of you have heard of John Ridley Stroop?'

He looks at Terence and Simon. Women are excluded from having heard of anybody, though Deborah has benefited from years of instruction. 'Stroop demonstrated that when the word for a colour – for instance, yellow – is printed in, for instance, blue, naming the colour on the page takes longer than when the colour of the ink and the word for the colour match. From what Debs tells me, this Child fellow reacts as though his *yellow* is always printed in *blue*. There is a significant time lag in his responses. I wonder whether drugs are causing the problem.'

'I think I have this Stroop thing,' Terence murmurs. 'Give or take a green or two.' He winks at me.

'Hang on. Just let me make my point and then you can talk away to your heart's content. Starting well is key. It establishes a virtuous circle.' Giles pauses as if to ascertain that we are familiar with the expression. 'When students fail it is invariably because they get behind. Catching up means fulfilling the previous demand and the latest one. Then along comes another. Before they know it they are snowed under. It is like debt accumulation, only the scarce resource is time not money.'

I worry for Jean, who, if still alive, will be stuck in the front basement room, waiting for this meeting to end so that she might nervously risk lighting a small cigar.

Cassie is fidgety. She has started to hum a belligerent little tune. She flexes her shoulders and stretches out her feet, revealing bare flesh between the end of her leggings and her fringed ankle boots.

Giles frowns at her. He clears his throat. 'In conclusion,

the man's not on the ball. It's crucial we act now. Not this time next January when it'll be too ruddy late. We've wasted enough time as it is.'

'I think he leaves the premises in the lunch hour,' Ginny says. 'Very unusual. I mean, there's nowhere to go, is there?'

Cassie stops humming. 'Cara's seen him in a tracksuit. He cycles. Bradley Wiggins, eat your heart out.'

'We can't hand out time, much as we'd like to.' Simon Petridis smiles sadly at her. 'But, with respect, these young people are not getting behind. They are failing to move forward. "Rewrite part of *Silas Marner* in the future." What kind of essay question is that?'

Simon is a full ten years older than the rest of us. His eyes are set in dark, baggy pouches. Their gaze has settled on the women in the group, each in turn. I felt pleasantly flattered when it happened to me, less so when he moved on to Deborah.

'And which future?' Terence asks. 'The 1890s, or nowadays, or some kind of sci-fi scenario?'

Deborah revs up. 'Typical of the man. Nothing is clear. You can be sure he isn't meeting his performance objectives. Goode won't divulge data concerning individual members of staff but he's told me the criteria: SMART. Specific, measurable, achievable, realistic and time-bound. Hurrah!'

'There is no rewind button,' Simon says.

'Action!' Deborah slaps her knees.

Giles bends down to put the empty bottle in the hearth and pick up a fresh one. He unscrews the cap.

'Lorna, you've been quiet. What's your take on the situation?' Ginny asks.

Light-headed from listening without taking part, I have a gulp of wine. I am tempted to share the information about the cupboard. Jude Bennet-Neerhoff has seen him go in there. They would fall on it and I would join the inner circle. I could use the word 'hide'. He hides in a cupboard. No, I do not know what he does in there. I imagine it's some kind of refuge. I would sound concerned. The kind of person who worries about the victim while offering him up. They are looking at me, expecting an answer.

'Ross is pretty silent on the matter. On most matters. I mean, how do you know all this stuff? Your children come home and talk?' I see from their expressions that the origin of my son's shortcomings is in my face. 'I'm against persecuting Alan Child,' I say. 'He's young. He's in his second year of teaching. He made a good start but it's all gone a bit flat. It happens. Maybe he'll fall for an Australian who pines for the sun and will transport him down under. There are usually plenty of Antipodeans at Lloyd-Barron Academy.'

'A touch fatalistic,' Terence says. 'The romantic solution.'

'Damned wishy-washy,' Giles snorts.

'Miss Robartes is fit. I think she's from South Africa,' Simon says.

'Watch it, Simon. We didn't hear that.' Deborah raises her eyebrows at him.

'I don't think anyone wants to persecute Mr Child, Lorna,' says Ginny. 'But it's in everyone's interests that complaints are resolved at the earliest opportunity.'

'He's a victimmy type.' Cassie holds out her glass. 'Just a small one, Giles. I'm driving. He should have been a librarian.'

'The first stage is informal, verbal or written,' Ginny says.

'Verbal. I'll do it.' Deborah bounces up from the sofa, causing Cassie and Ginny on either side to elevate too. 'If you need something done, ask a busy person.'

'Thank you, Deborah. Are we all happy with that?' We nod.

'Done!' Giles booms.

'I'll give you chapter and verse on the correct procedure,' Ginny says.

'Do you remember when Miss Bhimji played "The Last Post" and "The Rouse" on her tenor recorder to give emotional substance to the *Selected Poems of the First World War*?' Simon positions his fingers over the imaginary holes of an instrument. We fall silent.

24

'What is this?' Ross asks when I take the plum crumble from the oven.

'Crumble of the most basic sort. I used flour, white sugar, butter and plums. No rolled oats, flaked almonds, orange zest, pine nuts or any other additional ingredients. Help yourselves.'

'Looks like that leeks-and-breadcrumbs thing.'

'Gratin. It isn't. Why would I give you two main courses?'

'Short-term memory loss?'

He wolfs down the pudding and has a second helping.

'Sorry, Lorna. It's nice but I'm not hungry,' Jude says.

'It doesn't matter at all. Are you not feeling well?'

Jude pushes her spoon in and out of the mush on her plate.

'I keep thinking of Sadie.'

'Sadie?'

'Her dog, Mum. Catch up,' Ross says.

'I'm sorry. For no good reason, I thought of the dog as male.'

'What's that got to do with it?'

'Right at the beginning I envisaged two boys and a dog. You, Jude and, as it were, Jackson. It's disturbing that I see maleness as the norm. Three sons, a brother in Peterborough, a father, an ex-husband, my mother snatched from me by sudden cardiac arrest, my best friend in Aberystwyth – these are insufficient excuses.'

Jude's eyes fill with tears.

'Look what you've done, talking such drivel,' Ross says to me.

'I'm sorry, Jude.' I lean back, take the kitchen roll from the worktop and pass her a few torn-off sheets.

'Mum forgot to book up the kennels for the weekend. She remembered just as they were leaving. She called up but they were fully booked. 'Let's just *not* go,' she said which made Pappa furious. He said it was her responsibility to deal with the dog. She said it wasn't. In the end, she rang the hotel and asked if they could bring a dog and they said they could but they had to have a different, not-so-nice room. Poor Sadie. She hates long car journeys and she hates a bad atmosphere. There won't be anything for her to do in Manchester.'

'Oh dear. How difficult.'

She sniffs and wipes her face all over, as though drying a dish. 'Pappa doesn't care about Sadie and Mum doesn't care about any of us. She probably wishes we were dead. Then she'd be free to do whatever she wants.'

111

'And what does she—?' I begin.

'Mum. Please.'

'My father was married before. Pappa left Adrienne because of Mum. Now the shoe's on the other foot. Mum's having a relationship with someone at work.'

'An eye doctor?'

'Shut up,' Ross shouts as he rises from his chair.

'Yes. Dr Fred Grabowski.'

'I'm really sorry, Jude. It must be very upsetting for you,' I say.

Ross gives an exasperated sigh and subsides. He puts a protective hand on Jude's lower back.

'Mum was wearing a summer smock thing and an old white trench coat. Not even leggings. She'll be really cold. They both slammed the car doors and Pappa mashed the gears, driving off. He dropped me at the station. I was glad to get out of the car.' Jude snuggles into Ross. 'Do you want to finish my pudding?'

'Thanks, babe.' Ross holds her tight and begins to scoop up the mess on her plate.

'It'll work out, one way or another. They're going for couples' counselling,' Jude says.

They leave. The creaks of the bed are background noise, like rain on the roof or cars passing in the street. It is intolerable to register every footstep overhead, every banged door, the ebb and flow of recorded sound from one room or another. I sense as much as hear and resort to putting on the radio and turning up the volume to a level that indicates I have become deaf. In fact, I remind myself of my father who leaves Radio 3 on for company. Anything involving trumpets, he turns up to full blast. A Bach Brandenburg Concerto, for instance. I answer a message from Richard. I never see him at the weekend. He seems very far away.

25

I find my copy of *Silas Marner* in the bedroom cupboard, among belts and sunglasses that are no longer fashionable and letters from the days when people still wrote them. The book should have been returned to school and is still in the cellophane jacket that I covered it with in Upper Five, the corners stuck down on the inside with sticky tape that has become brittle and yellow. I remember the class listening in silence, stirring occasionally. Feet shuffled, a fingernail scraped on a desk, someone coughed; small elements of restlessness that, like the movement of a bird in a bush, have no power to disturb. As if willed by the group in front of her, our teacher, Miss Fletcher, rolled on, spellbound by the words and the good acoustic of a high-ceilinged classroom. '"She was perfectly quiet now, but not asleep – only soothed by sweet porridge and warmth into that wide-gazing calm which makes us older human beings, with our inward turmoil, feel a certain awe in the presence of a little child"' – the part where Godfrey Cass, having seen the face of his dead disowned wife, looks at his daughter cradled on Silas's lap, as he sits by the fire. The mystery of infancy and death persists through Silas and Godfrey's low-pitched conversation and Godfrey's return to the Red House. Even though the end-of-lesson hooter sounded, it persists. The peace of a baby radiates to fill a room, a whole house. Miss Fletcher carried on reading.

Outside it grows dark but nothing changes. At this time of year, the lights stay on all day. Ross and Jude sleep in. They do homework. They go for bike rides. Blandness, like a mild headache, takes hold, tinged with disappointment peculiar to Saturday afternoons in winter. I hope life in our house is not too dull for Jude.

I get out the Terry's All Gold to show her. It is the 16oz box and contains family photographs, not the early snaps of me and Randal, but pictures of the boys.

'You were really pretty, Lorna,' she says, 'and the little boys are so cute. You should put some of these out, make a collage or something.'

The television is on, though we are not paying it much attention.

'You don't have any photos on display, do you? Not even in your bedroom. Mum and Pappa have this long line along the radiator shelf.' She stretches her arms out. 'I like their graduation pictures, though they *are* silly. I'm

115

looking forward to mine. The gown and the hat. It's a shame Ewan never got that far.'

I stiffen but carry on shuffling through the box, passing her pictures I think she might like. She sits with one leg tucked under her, comfortable.

'Oliver and Ewan were a bit alike, weren't they?' Jude holds up a holiday snap of the two boys. She turns it this way and that and gazes into it as though into a make-up mirror. Her lean face turns rapidly to profile. All nose when her hair hangs loose and all cheekbone when she pushes it back.

'Those two are more Doig than Parry, though Oliver's fair like me and Ewan is dark.'

She carries on examining the photos. 'It's weird the way you talk to Ewan.'

'Weird in what way?' I say quickly.

'Sort of monotonous? As if you don't expect a reply?'

I take a deep breath. 'A soliloquy?' I say. 'I hadn't thought of it in those terms but maybe you're right. From Latin – *solus*, alone, and *loqui*, to speak.'

'I didn't know that. That's cool.'

'A series of reflections not meant to be overheard. The audience participates in the illusion.'

'The first time I heard you, you said something about a sick cat.'

I glance at the television screen. Elderly people in

wheelchairs are being entertained by a woman in Edwardian-style drag. I note the jauntily angled top hat and the striped waistcoat. Heads are thrown back in sleep or nodding on chests. One lady taps her fingers on the armrest in time to the music, though her eyes remain closed. I turn down the volume and we watch in silence for a few minutes. The camera focuses on another old veined hand as it wafts to and fro.

'Poor old things,' I say.

'Actually, Lorna, I thought he might be dead.'

Jude's phone beeps.

'It's Ross. He says to go back up. People do that, don't they? They carry on talking to someone who's died. And they keep the person's room as a kind of shrine,' she says.

'Usually tidier than Ewan's room. But that's terrible. Terrible that the thought crossed your mind. God, I can't believe it, Jude.'

'He must be so bored.' She seems lost in thought.

Upstairs, a door opens. 'Jude?' Ross calls out.

She deletes the message and pushes her phone towards me.

I peer at the screen. 'A box? What am I looking at?'

'It's an old-style reel-to-reel tape recorder. It's on the floor in that cupboard place I told you about. Remember, I said I'd find out what's in there.'

'They were built like tanks, those old recording machines. Impossible to lift. Everything that's now lightweight used to be heavy,' I say.

'I'm really surprised they leave the cupboard unlocked. They lock all the other rooms. I've seen Mr Child go in there a few times now.' Jude shows me close-up shots of a treasury tag and a black metal bulldog clip with its jaws clamped shut and the handles apart.

'Artistic,' I say. 'You could have an exhibition. *Still Lifes and an English Teacher*. So it was a stationery cupboard. Like you, Mr Child is too young to remember the valid use for a treasury tag.'

I think of Jude following him along the school corridor. And of Jude entering the unoccupied house at the end of the lane. The sign to the riding school and the horses warm and breathing in the darkness of their stalls.

On the television, a nurse is wheeling the drugs trolley. She pauses by one of the old women and hands her a little canister of pills and a beaker of water. The camera lingers on the nurse's watchful waiting. I imagine an agonised swallowing going on out of shot.

26

As I walk along Green Lanes, I glance down the Luptons' road at the unbroken terraces of houses. There is no one about. Cars are parked bumper to bumper on either side but the pavements lack shoppers. I go past boarded-up premises. I have lived into the late capitalist period and this is what it looks like. Kebab shops, fried-chicken shops, betting shops, pawnbrokers. No Woolworths. If cattle emerged from the quiet lines of an English print and lugged their heavy bodies in the direction of the North Circular, they would not cause much of a stir. The traffic is slow moving, as usual.

We look forward to meeting you, Dirk said. I wasn't keen to get involved but for Jude's sake I agreed. He suggested Palmers Green as the venue, though he and Frances do not know the area and I had to name the café. The choice was between the usual chains, one of the Greek Cypriot cake shops, or the bustling place with deliberately mismatching old china that is loved by young parents and crammed with buggies. I chose Costa's, one of the Greek Cypriot cake shops, though now, recalling the air of melancholy that prevails and the elaborate wedding cakes in the window, I think I have made the wrong decision.

The glass-fronted counter at Costa's displays cakes and pastries but they could be fake because there is no smell of baking. I remember this characteristic as soon as I walk through the door. Baking, I conclude, as I did on a previous visit, must happen off the premises.

I am the first to arrive at a few minutes before eleven and choose a table midway down the café in the centre row. The air is cold and I feel a draught around my ankles. I take off my coat and hang it over the back of the chair but keep my scarf on. The other tables, bolted down in neat ranks, one behind the other, are unoccupied. I take a book from my bag and begin to read without much attention, glancing up every now and then, though no one comes in or goes out.

At ten past, the door opens and two men walk in, the first in work dungarees and heavy boots. The second, older man comes straight towards me. He is tall, wide-shouldered and fails to smile – forgetful or unfriendly – I do not know which yet. He wears a dark padded jacket. His close-cropped hair is of an unvarying grey. I bob up. He shakes me by the hand, remaining severe.

'Frances is riding. She says hello and is sorry not to see you. I think on this occasion she really is with the horses.'

He undoes the buttons of his coat and sits down opposite me. His face shows signs of fatigue but I can see Jude in him. The sturdy set of the head, the downward-sloping eyes. The woman in the white wraparound overall comes out from behind the counter. We order coffee and Dirk gets up to choose a cake. He rises quickly and, before moving away, adjusts the position of his chair so that it is once more squared up with the table. After examining what is on offer and asking the woman various cake-related questions, he makes a decision.

'This is a good choice,' he says, as he sits down again. 'Quiet. A fragment of the past, like in a museum. When you said Costa's I thought no because I prefer to avoid the chains but then you said cake and I knew we were in business.' He puts his hands on the seat of the chair and repositions himself.

'It's rather cold in here. I'm sorry about that,' I say.

'Warmer than Manchester,' he says. 'The weekend there did not go well from my point of view. And Christmas was very difficult.'

'Ah,' I say, or perhaps it is some other indeterminate sound.

I tell him how much I like Jude. What a lovely girl she is. He clasps his hands together and bangs them against his lips. I ask him about his work. The conversation is hard going. I am aware of its construction – the

121

my turn, your turn. The gaps are like amnesia, or blank pages caused by a print error. I tell him – in some desperation – that my mother underwent tests for glaucoma when her optician noted that the pressure in her eyes was raised. The hospital appointment – just a few weeks before she died – was at eight in the morning and she spent most of the day in the waiting room, first reading a book, then, once eye drops were administered, no longer able to read; after every intervention, back among the other patients in the rows of chairs, waiting for a doctor or a machine to become available. She returned home elated, not caring at all about the time spent, because she was given the all-clear and did not have a lifetime of eye medication ahead of her.

'I see,' Dirk says, though I can tell he has stopped listening and closed an invisible door. I observed a similar expression on Randal's face when Jehovah's Witnesses called round with *The Watchtower* and tried to interest him in Armageddon.

'She always told a good story, putting on the voices and leaving out the tedious parts.'

'Good.' Dirk speaks curtly.

He fixes me with his gaze. There are fishtails at the corners of his eyes, where Jude's skin is smooth.

'I had thought we would reconnect in Manchester, or at least find some clarity. But there is no clarity. Yet. The weekend did not go well. Frances referred to many of my failings. Some general, some particular. The particular I didn't always recognise.' Dirk touches the little bowl of wrapped sugar with his fingertips and pushes it a few inches along the table as if making a chess move. 'She remembered things I said, even whole events, which I have no recall of at all. She spoke of an occasion in a shop in Biarritz when she was trying on a pair of trousers. There was another when we were on board a Stena Line ferry from Harwich to the Hook. I believe her because why should she make it up? I am perplexed that I have forgotten so much. It is like the *mise en abyme*. I am searching the long corridors of mirrors, looking for something I recognise. I don't even recall we went to Biarritz. The holiday in the Pays Basque, yes. Saint-Jean-Pied-de-Port where we stayed, the houses dipped in the River Nive, the cobbled main street, the very nice auberge where we ate colombe. From Saint-Jean-Pied-de-Port to Biarritz is many kilometres. Frances did not like to drive the big car on mountain roads and at that time I had a bad back. A sciatica for which I took painkiller. I had a seat wedge and an adjustable backrest made of basket. I would never have undertaken the journey.'

The woman comes out again from behind the counter. She brings two cups of coffee and a custard tart for Dirk on a thick white plate. I thank her. Dirk nods and bites into the puff pastry. He brushes the flakes from his lips.

'If her recollections are correct – and I have no reason to disbelieve her – I am indeed a monster. Such a person would cause unhappiness and the unhappiness would lead inevitably to Dr Fred Grabowski, a young, excessively handsome doctor who specialises in lacrimal surgery. Handsome to the point of ugliness. Or some similar man. Dr Fred Grabowski happened to be there at the right moment. The wrong moment for me. Often, it is the male who strays. When it is the woman it is doubly difficult because of the surprise element. I believed implicitly that Frances was where she said she would be. Tuesday evening at her clinic, Saturday morning with the horses. Where are people when they are not with you? Where do they go? I find I am questioning the most basic notions. Where is Mr Doig, for instance? I hope for your sake he is where he says he is. Now Dr Fred Grabowski has emerged and Frances has promised to tell the truth, however unwelcome, I believe she is where she says she is. There would be no advantage to a second layer of dishonesty at this point.'

His assertion is a form of words or comforting logic that has no bearing on the situation. He and Frances are pressed too close to it. Emotions whir like rotor blades: metal and air, false and true, are indistinguishable. When

124

the amount of lift produced by the speed exceeds the weight of the situation, they will grow lighter and slowly leave the ground. This may take months.

I hear the semi-jocular tone which at first I mistake for comedy but soon gather is a question of intonation and excellent but non-native English – this coupled with dejection. Dirk looks through rather than at me, seeing the scenes that overwhelm him, his mind mentally stretched almost beyond endurance to a point where he cannot control the flood of words, or the pace at which he delivers them. I continue to maintain eye contact – it is the least I can do – and take comfort from the solid items that edge my field of vision. The glass-fronted counter, the paper napkins in an aluminium container, the eclairs and meringues, the little pink-and-white pyramids that are tough on the teeth and in my childhood were called coconut kisses. I resign myself to the role of sap-head and follow pretty much until the point when Dirk says 'Mr Doig'. Then the transmission that has been coming in smoothly jerks to an unscheduled stop. Dirk Neerhoff hopes *for my sake* that Randal is where he says he is. I understand that Ross might never speak of Charmian – a name I avoid myself – but the sadness of this near-stranger believing that Ross's father still lives with us washes through me.

Dirk stirs his coffee, though he has not added sugar, and licks the spoon before repositioning it on the saucer.

He is staring at me, wanting, I can tell, more on his wife. Nothing about his daughter. Nothing about the teachers of Lloyd-Barron Academy. He hopes for an interim verdict.

I shift in my chair, aligning my spine with its back. 'She's still at home – Frances. She hasn't left. That's a good thing.'

'In theory, yes, but we must untie the knot when we are the knot – that is not so easy.'

'Isn't that always the dilemma?' I put as much brightness into my voice as I can manage. 'It's very hard for you. And very hard for Jude. How's she coping?'

'To be honest, she is vile. To both of us. And she cries. Have you heard her cry?'

'No.'

'Hmm. They are unstable in that age group. It is part of the territory.' He gives himself a little shake. 'Now we must speak of other things. I have talked only of myself and you will be thinking, Who is this selfish Dutchman? Maybe another cake would be nice.'

27

'I saw your dad. It was nice to meet him.'

'I knew Mum wouldn't go.'

'No?'

Jude is thinner. The marriage staggers on, it seems; efforts are made. She does not want to speak about the situation. I do not know if she can talk to Ross. They are still finding out about each other. Their chatting is sometimes easy, sometimes sticky as they enter a zone where one of them suddenly feels undefended. I notice moments – in-between moments when the music is off and she and Ross haven't decided what to do next – when Jude looks lonely. She is whippy like a sapling but vulnerable. I worry for her.

The pattern of Jude's visits becomes more erratic. Late arrivals on Friday. Early departures on Saturday. I do not know what's going on. The old regime has changed and is not balanced by Ross taking himself off to Crews Hill. In February half-term week, Jude does not show up.

'Is everything all right?' I ask Ross.

'Is everything all right?' he repeats in a speeded-up voice like a chipmunk.

'Well, is something wrong?'

'Nuh-hah.'

'What does that mean?'

Ross half in, half out of his room, jiggles the door to and fro while I talk so that for part of the time he disappears and I am speaking to chipped paint on wood. The light from inside comes and goes and this adds to the strange visual effect. I endure these background distractions without comment though I often feel like Trilby to the boys' Svengali and perform the role of mother in an amnesiac trance.

'Have you seen Jude? Are you going to Crews Hill?'

'Nuh-hah.'

'So you're not seeing her this weekend?'

'Nuh-hah.'

'Why's that?'

'She's got coursework.'

'And have you not got coursework? I haven't noticed you doing any.'

I spend too much time on the landings, talking at or through doors. This is one reason why nothing gets done in the house. Twenty years ago, I painted the walls teal, mustard and plum. The surfaces are scarred from fights and indoor ball games. The colours have faded. Randal

128

and I bought the walnut-veneered table at an antiques fair at Hatfield and later a red leatherette, stubby-legged sofa. After that we did not make much effort with the thirties look. I uncovered a parquet floor in the hall and passage when I took up the previous owners' carpet and then we inflicted damage on it in various ways. Although they were told not to, the boys used to race their toy cars down the stairs and, on different occasions, I dropped a hammer, a bottle of wine and a cast-iron pan of beef stew.

About a year before he left, Randal began to speak of plans for the house. A side-return extension. Replacement windows. They were little cameos of a distant moneyed future, made possible by the new job. He dropped them into the conversation. On one occasion, he mentioned adaptations to the house post-retirement – whether it would be possible to fit a stairlift when the stairs were so narrow. We were in the middle of dealing with a starling that had fallen down the living-room chimney. I love this house, he said. I don't want to leave it. What are you talking about? I said. We're years off retirement. Let's just get this poor bird out of the hall. The flapping is intolerable. The front door was open and the back door but the bird kept flying up, up and then down again, with a strong, direct flight. Its wingspan widened in the confined space. I could not bear the mad flying. I thought it would never end and that the half-crazed creature would carry on long into the evening; a perverted, one-bird version of the aeronautic starling displays that form ever-changing shapes and darken the sky.

Frances Bennet is forty-six. She is having or has had an affair with Dr Fred Grabowski. I see her, I do not know why, with her hair hidden under a towel arranged like a turban. I subtract from Jude's face those elements that belong to Dirk Neerhoff and am left with the nose and the cheekbones.

28

One Friday, Jude is back. She comes down for supper in a white blouse, black skirt and cardigan. Her hair is brushed and shiny. I never see her in her school uniform. She looks young. Though the clothes are the regulation monochrome, and abide by the sixth-form dress code, I can see that they are not the same as the other girls'. The shirt is made of stretchy fabric and Jude does up the buttons. This emphasises her breasts. The skirt is pleated. She displays a lot of leg, choosing to wear ankle socks in winter. She is exotic. She has not conformed.

'School attire. What's going on?' I say.

'Oh, I couldn't be bothered to go home and change.'

She appears in the kitchen the next morning, identically dressed. I put down the book I am reading, tighten the belt of the old towelling dressing gown with loops hanging off it and sit up straight. It is seven-thirty in the morning.

'Saturday, isn't it?' I say.

'Detention.' Jude takes two bowls out of the cupboard

and pours cornflakes into them, then milk to the brim of each bowl.

'Aren't you too old for that?' I get up to put the kettle on again.

She is preoccupied and does not respond. She sits down on a chair with her back to me.

'Jude?'

'They've added consolidation to the Performance framework. It's the new commitment policy. It runs all the way through the academy like a golden thread.'

'Their words, obviously?'

'What's she on about? Stop talking. We're in a rush.' Ross comes in, also in school uniform, shirt buttons undone, tie hanging loose round his neck. He pushes past me.

I notice a charred patch of tomatoey stuff on the stove. The seeds have turned into burnt ants. I begin to scrub at them with a cloth. 'Which part of the golden thread have you severed? Sit down, Ross.' I hand him a spoon.

'We haven't done anything wrong,' Jude says. 'It's work catch-up. We've got behind.'

'In English?'

'Yes, but Mr Goode organised it.'

'A penile collection.' Ross shovels cereal into his mouth. 'They have them at Oxford colleges.'

'Penal, surely?' I say. 'Does Mr Goode claim to have gone to Balliol?'

Ross has raised his head and is looking at Jude with a gaze that would disturb an animal. Then he catches me watching. 'For God's sake. Are you so ignorant?' he snaps.

'What time are you supposed to be there?' I say.

'Jude.' Ross gestures towards the door.

She stands up.

'See you later,' I say as she follows Ross out of the kitchen.

I hear the front door bang shut. I go upstairs and into the bathroom, carrying a mug of tea. The air is as wet and hot as a tropical greenhouse. It takes me a few seconds to register 'FUCK GOODE', written in the steam that has formed on the mirror. The words have already begun to drip so that the letters resemble the piratical writing of a message traced in blood.

I take off my dressing gown and hang it on the hook on the back of the door. I appear as a smudged red-and-grey blur in my winter pyjamas, more a colour palette than a person, with chinks of realism in the cleared spaces of lettering. I have never seen Jude's handwriting. It could be hers. The D resembles Ewan's D, a shallow backward C with a line that fails to meet the sides of the curve. Ross's is different, all joined up.

They have carved out distinctive styles in the repeated writing of Doig. I swish away the sudsy mound over the shower drain, pick up the towels that lie in a heap on the floor and open the window. The steam clears in the draught.

29

On my first inspection of the archive in Cheshire, I fantasised about a cavern with the documents shelved between salt pillars, since Winsford Rock Salt Mine used the 'room and pillar' method of mining that involved leaving supports to hold up the roof before the 'room' was relinquished and the miners moved on to a new area. In reality, the underground facility lacks romance. The store in the worked-out part of the mine houses not only the London Transport archive but also confidential government files, hospital patient records, business gen from private companies and part of the Bodleian Library. It has the benefit of naturally constant levels of humidity and temperature but is otherwise mundane, with walls, floors and ceilings no different from any other warehouse space. Boxes are stacked on high metal shelves and conform to British Standards. Although the mine was shut down in the late nineteenth century because of over-capacity in the salt industry, it reopened in the 1920s and is still operational. It stretches five kilometres east to west, and three kilometres north to south, and supplies rock salt to de-ice the roads of Britain in winter.

Storage is costly and I am gradually transferring data onto digital files. For the moment, tangible, musty-smelling proof of the past, including the heavy, bound staff registers that date back to 1863, remains in hard copy. So much has gone missing – from the ancient library of Alexandria to yesterday's travelcard dropped on the pavement; lost, discarded, burnt, blown up. The ordered shelving gives me pleasure.

I make the trip in a day. A two-hour train journey each way with a change at Crewe followed by a cab ride to and from the station out of town, along the River Weaver. Gradually, as the train travels further from London, the level of light rises and, looking out into the wash of grey, I feel as though I have taken a drug that allows me to see the unexceptional nature of the English landscape.

In the quiet zone, noise is at a minimum. Passengers tap on their electronic equipment in silent mode. From time to time, announcements over the intercom break in. I take out a book and when the train comes to a halt at a set of signals I look up. A tractor is moving slowly across a field.

There is no trolley service on the return journey so I go to the bar to buy a cup of tea. The train is packed with people visiting London or returning there for the weekend. While I wait in the queue, I check my phone and find a voice message from my father and a text from Ginny Lu. Both ask me to call them. I start with William. He is flustered. He says he won't be coming for lunch on Sunday. He apologises for giving such short notice and hopes I haven't already bought the food. The explanation he gives is that he is going to the National Army Museum to see 'a small exhibition on the Battle of Inkerman'. He clears his throat and adds, 'With Jane.' After the unenthusiastic, Oh, OK, with which I respond, he goes on to say that an ancestor of Jane's, of the 47th Regiment, distinguished himself on that occasion. I try to cut him short, fearing that what Ginny has to say involves Ross, but my father ploughs on, telling me of various outings that he and Jane have been on together. I interrupt him again. He gets the wrong end of the stick and seems to think I am on my way to a school do.

'Strange, all this fraternising with teachers that goes on these days,' he says. 'Father and I once bumped into the chemistry teacher at a rugby match at Twickenham. I was appalled to see the man out of context without his white coat on. It would not be a problem for me now. He'd say, "Hello William," and I'd think, Who the hell are you?'

By the time I get him off the phone I am too close to

the front of the queue to call Ginny. The man immediately ahead delves repeatedly in his trouser pocket for change to pay for two cans of extra-strong lager and a ham sandwich tight wrapped in cling film.

The woman who is serving glances at the money laid out on the counter. 'Another five p.' She pats her hair.

The man fishes again and the tiny coin that is stuck to his hand dislodges itself and rolls to the floor.

'Leave it. I'll look for it later,' the woman says.

He starts to bend down. 'Where's the blighter gone?'

'Leave it.'

He puffs as he straightens up, his face as dark and mottled as corned beef. He picks up the small paper carrier bag and goes over to the automatic doors.

'He can't see the button,' the woman says to me. 'It's got a bleeding light on. What can I get you, love? Press the button,' she calls out. 'Tea? Two pound fifty, darling. He needs his mother. There's plenty like him, I tell you. Help yourself to milk and sugar.'

The catering facility in Coach H is a forlorn place, part of the train but with the atmosphere of an outpost, somewhere rancid and enclosed, like a police cell. On the floor, older, ineradicable stains show through patches of newly spilt liquids. There is no window. Light bites and snacks on the racks might be all that is left in the world and constitute a last meal for a survivor who still has an appetite. I balance the poly-foam cup on one of the high perching tables, prise off the lid and add milk from the miniature carton. I have nowhere to put the floating teabag, though a stirring stick is provided. I jam the lid back on and call Ginny.

'Oh, Lorna.'

I grip the phone.

'Can I talk to you in confidence?'

'Yes, of course.'

'Ross isn't with you?'

'No, I'm on a train. Where is he? Is he all right?'

'Ross? Lorna, this is about Alan Child.'

Ginny's voice is quiet and precise. I miss some of what she says because a group of football supporters piles in through the automatic doors. Through barked-out chants and hollering, I get the gist of what she is saying.

139

30

I walk back through the swaying carriages, pressing buttons to allow my passage from one to the next. Differing levels of clamour cross my path. Each section produces its own blend of voices and bleeping. The train speeds along, seemingly lengthening as it goes, stretching to a distant northern county. I put in the miles. I pass luggage and passengers, more luggage, more passengers, and enter the quiet coach; its muffled hush hits me like a wall, as the doors sigh behind me. I return to my seat. Someone is sitting opposite, a young woman with hair dyed silvery grey. She is knitting.

Booking seats on a train is an unremarkable process – I did it myself – but the woman's appearance in my absence startles me. Wearing black, fashionably geeky spectacles and constantly moving her fingers over yarn and needles, she has replaced the white booking ticket on which was written 'Birmingham New Street/ London'. I have no recollection of the train having stopped while I stood in Coach H. No jolts, no sensation of rest. I failed to hear the announcements.

I remove the lid from the cup. The tea is mahogany coloured with creamy flecks on the surface where the milk has separated. I take a tissue from my bag, pull out the teabag by a corner, since I have mislaid the stick, and place it on the tissue. My hand is shaking. Immediately, a stain begins to spread and I hastily fold the tissue into a small disgusting parcel and dab at the table with it, meanwhile holding the cup with my other hand to stop it from spilling. The young woman continues to knit, breaking her rhythm only to yank more wool from the ball in her lap. My eyes are drawn to the soft yarn. It is a beautiful pebble-grey colour and so unspoiled that I can smell its newness. I gulp the tea down and, as soon as I have finished, drop the tissue parcel, by now soaked through, into the cup and replace the lid. I close my eyes to shut out the lighted carriage and the rushing dark.

The house smells of fried chicken. There are used cartons on the kitchen table, also my note to Ross about buying a takeaway. The money I left has gone. I hear voices upstairs and, every now and then, footsteps that cross the room. Jude is here. I clear away the rubbish, put forks and glasses in the dishwasher and, though it is frosty outside, I open the back door and stand for a few moments, wrapped in my coat and hugging my arms. No school until Monday. The head, who is not a reflective man, will have time to reflect. He can take advice on the best way to handle the situation. The important thing, from his point of view, is to control information.

Ginny asked me to uphold confidentiality. Naturally, I agreed. Our children should be in the same position as all the other students. There is a procedure to follow. A variety of groups must be informed in the right order: the governing body, the trustees, senior management, teaching staff, support staff, students in general, students in particular – those taught by Mr Child, or in his tutor group – parents. Ginny mentioned a Crisis Prevention Response Plan and I did not ask whether such a thing already existed or would be drawn up hastily on the back of an envelope over the weekend. It was not of great importance either way. Sometimes a crisis produces clearer thinking than a committee at ease.

I shut the door and take off my coat. I should eat, but the lingering smell in the kitchen nauseates me and combines with a memory of the train bar's beery stench. I go back through the thread of emails that followed the meeting at the Luptons' house. The first lot deals with dates; endless rescheduling as Deborah tries to fix up a meeting. She describes her assaults on the systems of Lloyd-Barron Academy, the passive aggression of Amrita, the head's secretary, the strategic diary clashes and last-minute cancellations. Other members of the parents' group responded. I took no part. Even when there was something concrete to discuss – an action plan to improve Mr Child's teaching – I let the comments pass me by as though they were poster ads next to an escalator.

How frustrating. Predictable but then I'm cynical. Surprise, Surprise. A CLASH? Do none of them keep a diary?? We don't want this thing to drag on. Fingers Xed sonny boy shows up. What are the chances? My guesstimate no better than 50/50. Don't forget to mention negativity. Too vague, Simon. Stick to competence specifics. Still on Silas Marner? *(YAWN) How long is it? Something more upbeat next time please. Good luck Deborah Good luck Deborah Good luck Debs. Good evening one and all. The deed is done. This is the action plan. We covered the following bullet points, 1–8. Looks good to me. V. clear. Well done, Deborah. Excellent result. Move speedily on to Stage 2 if he doesn't deliver. Great idea to have after-school coaching. Holidays too?? Keep the pressure on. Thanks Deborah Thank you Thankyou.*

I feel unsteady, as if still in motion.

31

The next morning I wake at four-thirty on the dot. I lie in bed for the first hour, then can stand immobility no longer and get up. Downstairs, in the kitchen, I make tea, read a book and from time to time glance through the window at the quiet garden and the sky above the rooftops to see if it is getting light. For warmth I switch on the oven and leave the door open. The little blue flames flicker and a smell, part gassy, part reheated baked food, drifts out. I feel disconnected from the rest of the house. The sleepers on the floors above are nothing to do with me. Jude, Ross, Ewan. It is as if I and they exist in different dimensions. The central heating comes on. I switch the oven off and go upstairs to have a bath and get dressed. I listen to the radio but I cannot settle.

Later, I drive to the supermarket to stock up for the week. Up and down the aisles I field the trolley. Vegetables. Fruit. Half a leg of lamb for Sunday lunch. Colleague announcement: Please will . . . Packs of minced beef. Bread. I walk past pyramid displays of Easter eggs. Sorry, could I just . . . Cheese. Ham. Milk. Yoghurt. In it all goes. Excuse me. Pasta. Breakfast cereal. Excuse me, are you in the queue? Beep. Beep. Please wait for assistance. I've no idea why . . . OK, thanks. The bill is enormous. Feed us until next Saturday.

As I pass the living room, a piece of paper flutters and catches my eye. Jude is at the table, an open book, her laptop and a pad of A4 in front of her, some loose sheets, some screwed up in balls. I put the bags of food shopping down in the hall and go in to say hello. I give her a sideways hug. I can feel the bones in her shoulder.

'Is everything all right? You don't usually work down here.'

'I've got this timed essay to write. It's quite difficult.'

'History? For Mrs Anstey?'

'No, English, for Mr Child. I don't really know what I'm doing. So far it's rubbish.' Jude indicates the screwed-up paper.

'Can I help?'

''S'all right.' She tugs at the bottom of the large sweatshirt that belongs to Ross and which she wears as all-purpose leisurewear. 'Lorna?'

'Mm?'

'I've reset the start time twice already. Mr Child won't know, will he? Does it matter?'

'No. It doesn't matter at all.'

145

Jude bends her head. She turns over the pages of the book.

'Just do your best,' I say and leave her.

I go out into the garden. A pair of blue tits on the bird feeder startle and fly away. When Mr Milner found out that Mr Child had missed his afternoon classes he and two senior members of staff went to look for him. Police arrived at the school and also an ambulance. Lessons had ended. The students gone. Staff off to the pub. Most of them. On a Friday. There are no extracurricular activities at the end of the week.

In the after-shock of sirens, the nearby roads fell quiet. The one-decker buses bowled along empty of passengers; floors and seats littered with empty drinks cans and food wrappers, single items of school uniform, a blazer or a tie, chewing gum stamped like grey rounds of sealing wax. Mr Milner, back in his office, resumed marking. The head left. It was his wife's birthday. Dinner was booked and, later on, the theatre.

32

In mid-afternoon, the doorbell rings. I am puzzled by the silhouette behind the glass in the front door. A courier, I think, though I have no idea what the delivery might be.

'Hi, Lorna.' Randal, in biker's leathers, on the doorstep, is removing his helmet.

'Good heavens,' I say.

'My new toy. It's a fantastic way of travelling. All the advantages of a car and a bicycle. Please don't make the inevitable references. I kept calling to let you know I was coming but you didn't pick up.'

'Oh, I switched my phone off. I had a nap. You look like one of those knightly ghosts that carries its head under its arm.'

He puts the helmet on the floor, takes off his gauntlets and begins to peel off his outer clothing. For a few seconds, I watch, mesmerised, then, as he steps out of the trousers, collect myself. 'I'll go and make some tea,' I say.

I hear his steps on the stairs. A muffled interchange

takes place with Ross, then Randal goes up to the top of the house. I listen for the knock on Ewan's door.

He stays up there for about fifteen minutes.

'Ross says they'll be down later. Jude says hi. Nice girl, isn't she?'

I turn the radio off and we go into the living room. I place Randal's mug of tea on the floor by the sofa.

'Ewan seems brighter,' he says.

'Brighter?'

'Yeah. I mean, he's not particularly communicative, but his face. It struck me as brighter.'

'That's great. Would I notice tiny changes? I don't know. I'm happy to believe you.'

'But *you* look tired, Lorna. Are you all right?'

'I woke up too early. I'm fine.'

'How early?'

'Four-thirty?'

'Oh, not too bad. I thought you were going to say two. We were up and down with Stefan. You know what toddlers are like with a cold. His nose was blocked, poor little sod.'

A car alarm starts; a prolonged hoot.

Randal picks up his mug and sips cautiously. 'Normal tea. Thanks.'

We chat until Ross and Jude come down. She is still wearing the sweatshirt – her breasts comfortably free inside the capacious garment – but she has put on a pair of black leggings. Usually she wanders round the house with bare legs. Ross is wearing an old tweed cap knocked to the back of his head. They both carry their phones and, in addition, Jude clasps her copy of *Silas Marner*. There is an element of constraint, as though they are about to put on a home-made play. The staged but sheepish entrance. The devastating pause in which it dawns on the actors that even improvisation requires a plan. Randal, Helena, William and I used to watch from a mock-up auditorium of sofa and two rows of dining chairs, our tickets ready for inspection. Shields and weaponry came from the kitchen. Bath towels were borrowed as togas. The performances involved fighting and were over quickly. On one less Roman occasion, Oliver went into labour with a lot of grunting and Ewan, the doctor, assisted with various pieces of garden equipment that he drew with a mixture of desperation and excitement from an old string bag: a trowel, a garden sieve, a packet of sunflower seeds and a ball of twine.

'How's the homework going?' I ask Jude.

'Terrible.'

'We can't stay long. Jude hasn't finished,' Ross says.

'Well, at least sit down. Don't you have to write this timed essay thing too?' I say.

'I'll do it tomorrow when Jude's gone. Only takes an

hour.' Ross drops down on the floor in front of the fire-place, Jude next to him.

'Where's that from?' I ask, tapping my head.

'Where's what from?' Ross says.

'The headgear.'

'Cap. Not headgear. Why do you always think you're Jane Austen, or something? I found it up the road. On a post.'

I cannot begin to put right the misconceptions contained in his question. But for a few seconds it distracts me.

Randal laughs. 'She is annoying, isn't she? What is the terrible essay?'

'We have to analyse a passage in *Silas Marner* and explain its significance to the work as a whole,' Jude says.

'I hope it has some. Significance, I mean. Does it?' Randal asks.

'Oh, yes.' Jude's expression is serious. 'I could read it to you, if you like?'

'Yes, please go ahead,' Randal says.

Jude, who is still sitting on the floor, puts her hair behind her ears, opens the book and holds it in two hands, like a chorister. She clears her throat.

'"Thought had been very busy in Eppie as she listened to the contest between her old long-loved father and this

150

new unfamiliar father who had suddenly come to fill the place of that black featureless shadow which had held the ring and placed it on her mother's finger. Her imagination had darted backward in conjectures, and forward in previsions, of what this revealed fatherhood implied; and there were words in Godfrey's last speech which helped to make the previsions especially definite."'

Randal gazes at Jude as she reads. Her face, the young body under the skull-print fabric, the slender ankles in overlarge socks. I wonder whether he would look at her like that if he lived here. He reveals more than fatherhood. She is seventeen years old, the daughter of doctors. One day, she may have to meet Fred Grabowski. She glances up, aware of Randal, then she looks back down at the text. Ross traces pictures in the rug with his fingers.

'Hmm,' Randal says when she finishes. 'I'd have to hear it again before making any useful comment. You read well.'

'We have to say what kind of paragraph it is. Coordinate, subordinate or mixed sequence,' Jude says.

'Very erudite. Is that what's called New Criticism?' Randal says.

'Is it, Lorna?' Jude asks.

'I think New Criticism is old hat now,' I say.

'Perhaps your teacher is old. My age. Is she?' Randal

emphasises the word 'old' jokily. From Jude, he hopes for a disclaimer.

'He,' I say. 'Mr Child.'

'He's quite young, I think. Would you like to see him?' Jude puts the book down, picks up her phone and goes over to Randal.

'Is that one of the pictures you showed me?' I say quickly.

'No. This is a new one. I took it yesterday.'

Randal, who pretends he does not need reading glasses, moves Jude's hand so that the phone is in a better position for him to be able to see. 'He seems to be carrying a chair.'

'Yes,' Jude says. 'He goes into this cupboard place – an old stationery cupboard – and we don't know what he does in there. Lorna said maybe mindfulness training – or erotic asphyxiation.'

'Did she, indeed?' Randal shoots me a glance of mock astonishment. 'I'm enjoying this.'

'I never said that. Surely not?'

Randal dismisses me with a gesture. 'Funny you should mention mindfulness. We had a taster session of it at work the other week. It went down well. I was surprised. We might roll it out across the company – purchase the downloadable MP3 and get everyone practising the technique. But back to your teacher and

Lorna's astonishing conjecture. What kind of person is he? Do you like him?'

'He doesn't have much personality,' Jude says. 'And he's no good at explaining things.'

'A black featureless shadow, eh? Carrying a chair and a small rucksack. I'm more prosaic than Lorna. She has a wild imagination. I think he was going to change the light bulb. What do you say to that?'

Ross groans. 'Don't start him on light-bulb jokes. He tells the most terrible jokes.'

'How big is this cupboard?' Randal asks.

I see silver stars above the fireplace. They are linked in a string and draped over the mirror. One end of the string starts to lift as though something or someone tugs at it. The sparkly thread moves in a slow, sick circle and the room is dragged along too, like a curtain on a rail. The pictures slip between the folds of the walls, then the windows. They are dark, glassy squares that slide away and reappear. When the furniture leaves the floor I put my head between my knees into upside-down dark.

Lorna. Mum. Voices break through. I am light. I am heavy as a bell. Inside my skull, matter spins and tips, spins and settles.

I bring myself cautiously to a vertical. Three faces. They tip backwards and forwards. I try to smile, though my lips are dry and the shape they make feels lopsided and far from reassuring. I must have missed the stars when I took the Christmas decorations down. The spot is out of reach of a tall man or boy, even should one be willing. A stepladder is required. The box marked 'Brother' has been put away.

33

I switch the oven on and go to the fridge to get out the shoulder of lamb. As I sit the meat on the rack of the roasting pan, I remember that William is not coming for Sunday lunch, a fact I forgot as I threw food into the supermarket trolley – and at every point until this moment. I am sorry I won't be seeing my father. I want to take his coat from him in the hall, let it hang over my arm – its weight a comfort – while we greet each other and go through the normal enquiries. Health, journey, sons and so on. Apart from the corduroy suit that he wears for special occasions, he sticks to a plain cotton shirt of indeterminate grey/green colour, beige trousers held up by a brown leather belt, a wool jacket and one of a selection of crew-necked jumpers darned at the elbows and cuffs by my mother. He washes with a kind of soap that no one buys any more. The peppery cologne smell of the soap is particular to him and I am glad that he bothers to make the journey to the chemist's shop in Cricklewood that still stocks it. I lead the way to the kitchen. He sits at the table and I pour him a drink. You're hovering, he says. Anything I can do? No, you just sit there, Dad, and enjoy your wine. I resume chopping the parsley, or whatever it happens to be, surprised, as I always am when my father first arrives, that time is at a standstill.

The back gardens are quiet on a Sunday morning. The sky is the same white as on the previous day, sterile and dazzling. I check my messages in case there is something more from Ginny.

Around midday, there are stirrings upstairs; music, doors slammed, feet, the sound of the shower going. Soon afterwards, Jude calls out goodbye and leaves for Crews Hill. I imagine Jane Brims and William plodding round the National Army Museum in their outdoor clothes; two seniors with their concession tickets. My earlier, manic animosity towards the woman has dulled.

'Grandad's not coming today,' I tell Ross when he comes down for roast lamb. 'He's gone to an exhibition.'

'Oh, OK.'

'With a friend. Jane Brims.'

'Nice.'

Ross has never heard of the Crimean War so I give him a short, possibly not wholly accurate résumé of events and recite some of Tennyson's poem, 'The Charge of the Light Brigade'. He seems to tolerate this, and I assume he is not listening, but at the end he says, 'You said "not" twice.'

'That's right, "not Not the six hundred".'

'So that means they all came back. All six hundred of them. What's the fuss about?' His mouth is full of roast potato.

We argue for about fifteen minutes. It is like talking to Bishop Lowth. I come close to raising the Chapter Sixteen, sixteen-years controversy that Deborah Lupton mentioned but stop myself. The ramifications are complex – too many sixes, like the mark of the Beast – and I have the information third hand.

'Why didn't you go to the exhibition as well, if you're so interested?' he says.

'Fair comment,' I say.

34

I signed up for ParentMail years ago. The letter when it comes, late on Tuesday afternoon, is electronic. The content and style are peculiarly bloodless and the tone is wrong. I am used to the garbled messages that emanate from the school: the mixture of management-speak and muddled syntax that through obfuscation – deliberate and accidental – reveals a holier-than-thou defensiveness that sickens me. They are, it seems, always hiding something. My father, who believes in a good-quality sealed envelope and headed writing paper, would blame the medium, and perhaps, in this instance, he would be right. There is a lack of respect in the paragraph that pops into my inbox under the strap-line, *Important Announcement.*

The writer, or committee of writers, has taken pains to give as little information as possible. The result is puzzling. I am left wondering whether Mr Child succumbed to a sudden mysterious illness or was involved in a road-traffic accident in the vicinity of the academy. Nothing bad happens on the premises. A casual reader might think he was alive but unable to continue in his chosen profession. Having dealt with the tragedy, they move on to school housekeeping:

> *Miss de Silva, who many of you know but many of you might not know that she has a joint honours degree in Theology and English Literature, will put on her other hat and be taking the Year 12 English group until a new, permanent member of staff is appointed. Excellent temporary staff under the expert guidance of Mrs Sharon Laws will be covering Years 7 to 11. You should be assured that recruitment has already begun. We mustn't forget that the period we had the leaks was in an exceptionally inclement period and an overkill situation should be avoided not withstanding it may be pragmatic to bite the bullet as a long-term solution.*

To close, the standard spiel about the school's counselling service is pasted in.

'This is very sad news about Mr Child.'

Ross, at his desk, has his back to me. The curtains are open and in the reflections of the glass I see the lid of his laptop, the blue of his sweatshirt, part of his face.

'What about him?'

'Well, he's died, Ross, hasn't he?'

Ross makes some kind of noise, possibly of assent, if not confirmation.

'I've had an email from school.'

'There you go.'

'Are they marking it in some way?'

'What?'

'A special service or assembly.'

'Prayers, you mean?'

'Maybe but not necessarily. It wouldn't have to be religious as such.'

'There's no such thing as non-religious prayers. "O Mr and Mrs Child, we remember today your son, Alan Child."'

'Ross, that's horrible. His poor parents. Anyway, he might not have any.'

'Yeah, he lives with them. In Romford. Why doesn't he get his own place?'

'Lived. Didn't. Don't keep using the present tense. It's really unpleasant. What's the matter with you?'

'He's too old to live at home. Was, sorry.'

'I think you're being incredibly callous. What's got into you?'

Beyond and through the mirrored bedroom are the lighted windows of the next street's houses and the dark outlines of roofs with their redundant chimney stacks. In the intermediate space the tree's branches hold steady

– they stretch in every direction – and invade the shadow copy of my son.

'Is Jude OK?'

No response.

'Is she?'

He nods, grudgingly. I wait. He flings out an arm. It is a gesture of dismissal but I stay put.

'Why are you still there?' he says after several seconds have passed.

'We haven't finished the conversation.'

'There isn't a conversation.'

'She wasn't her usual self at the weekend.'

No response.

'It won't be easy for her. Her mum and dad with their troubles. And now this sad thing at school.'

35

'Doing anything nice this evening?' my hairstylist asks. Her name is Dahlia and she comes from Estonia.

'No, nothing special.' My upper chest is weighed down with a heavy rubber cutting collar, a curious fetishistic object that some people might enjoy but the sensation reminds me of the bouts of bronchitis I suffered from every winter in my cigarette-smoking days. Underneath is a billowing black nylon cape without slits for hands. I am entrapped in this costume with only my head showing, like Estelle, the fairground spider woman, who wrecked any illusion that she was a phenomenon of nature by chatting to us from her web and asking my brother, Hugh, and me our names and ages and what we liked doing at school. I believed that she and Electra, who defied death by 27,000 volts, were wholly contemporary though they must have been vintage artistes in that era – revivals several times over – like the steam fair rides, and billed as such in garish posters. The headless lady was my favourite. She stood at a counter with a mirror behind her, like the woman in Manet's painting,

A Bar at the Folies-Bergère. You could see the back of her velvet dress and the bow of her white apron. She poured drinks for imaginary customers and for the intoxicating climax of the act made as if to take a surreptitious snifter herself. She raised the glass to absent lips. My eyes never left her. In the last crucial second, before the red wine vanished into thin air, or alternatively spilled down her front, her shoulders twitched, as though she sensed the landlord watching nearby, thought better of the action, diverted the glass, and lifted it in a toast to the audience.

I forget. And then I remember again. It is a relief, though, to get rid of this hair.

'Any plans for the weekend?' Dahlia rapidly tugs a combful of strands to ninety degrees and snips.

'No. No, nothing particular is happening. It's just a normal weekend.'

'That is good too. If you don't have to work, you can put your feet up. Relax.'

I smile.

The door is constantly opening and shutting as people walk in from Victoria Street. The radio is tuned to Kiss FM and the stylists, who are never the same from one visit to the next, stand over their clients with flickering scissors. They wear black close-fitting dancers' clothes and cut to the offbeat. Cordless trimmers buzz. Blasts of

163

hairdryer air blow like crosswinds. Clumps of my hair fall to the floor. My face, more and more exposed, appears – there is no escaping from it – tired and aged, both in repose and when I move my lips in reply to Dahlia. I keep my head rock still.

I no longer wish for a continuing relationship with my hairdresser, of the sort I once had with Greg in Verve of Palmers Green who cut the boys' hair and Randal's too and knew all our names. He had a soft Dublin voice. Greg would never have supposed that I would spend the weekend with my feet up, as he knew all too well, from my fruitless attempts to stop my sons from darting about the salon and fighting each other and from Randal's interminable accounts of sporting activities designed to use up surplus boy energy, that we rarely sat down. At a later stage, when the boys were older and slunk in unaccompanied, he understood that our difficulties were by no means over.

I am aware that, having failed to provide verbal evidence of a man with whom I shall go clubbing or out for a nice meal, Dahlia has me down for a sad middle-aged singleton, perhaps with a cat. I cannot complain, having opted out of an ongoing hairdressing association by coming to a salon that is the hair equivalent of fast food. I stopped going to Greg without warning and occasionally wonder if *he* wonders what happened to us, five people – two adults, three children – who, after several years of cheerful interconnection, between one month and the next disappeared from the face of the earth without saying goodbye.

36

Ginny calls me on Thursday morning and asks to meet up. She sounds tearful. I offer to travel to somewhere near her place of work, if she can suggest a suitable venue, but she insists that she comes to me, so we settle on The Albert, on Victoria Street, at six-thirty p.m. No one there will know us.

We arrive at the same time and head for an unoccupied corner on the far side of the bar, where Richard Watson and I often sit when we meet for a drink. The clientele is a mix of tourists and local office workers. The two groups tolerate each other but have no connection. The one soaks up the atmosphere created by the mahogany bar counter, the decorative etched-glass windows and the portraits of British prime ministers that line the walls, the other sloughs off the day's troubles.

We extricate ourselves from our coats and stow bags and wet umbrellas – a procedure that takes longer than when I was young. Ginny settles herself on a Windsor chair and I go to the bar to buy drinks.

'Oh, Lorna, I should have done it myself,' she says,

the second I return. She takes a large gulp of red wine. I have never seen her so agitated.

'Done what, Ginny?' I ask.

'Initiated the complaints procedure. You know what Deborah is like. The head . . .' She wafts her free hand.

'Is incompetent. Out of his depth. He's a windbag. All that golden-thread consolidation bollocks. Who writes that terrible stuff? The building manager? The latest email was a shocker.'

'Oh, Lorna. We should have gone more gently. You were right.'

I am dazzled by the unexpected endorsement but hate to see Ginny distressed. In her neat, girlish clothes and with a fringe as straight as a high-tensile fence, she does not suit anguish. I tell her she mustn't blame herself.

Ginny clasps her hands together. 'I'm so used to Deborah, I forget the impact she has. If you are feeling crushed . . . And not just poor Mr Child. She has this authority, so in order to assert himself, the head becomes, well, I probably shouldn't say this – but cruel. He has it in him to be cruel. He probably leant on poor Mr Child very hard.'

'She is also a bit of a comedy act, Deborah. You wouldn't necessarily take her seriously.'

'But what could be more serious than this?'

I nod. 'No. Nothing.' I rip the top off the packet of

167

dry-roasted peanuts with my teeth and pass it to Ginny. She dips in and puts a few nuts in her mouth, chasing them down with a swig of wine as though swallowing aspirin. 'He lived with his parents. In Romford. Such a difficult commute. Sometimes he borrowed his mother's car. Mostly he cycled. All that way.' She pauses. I wait. Ginny dips into the peanuts and repeats the prophylactic swig. 'He stopped going to the staffroom at lunch-time. A group of teachers were very unkind to him. Nesta Robartes should have kept her mouth shut.' Ginny presses her lips into a line, as if enacting how Miss Robartes should have behaved. 'You know who I'm talking about?'

'Simon Petridis mentioned her. I've never come across her.'

'She's a science teacher, new this year. From South Africa. Very pretty. She is one of those girls with trans-lucent skin – almost blue under the surface. Grey eyes. Her hair is curly, the colour of wheat. She seems to be half-asleep. She *looks* half-asleep. She plays a *wot*.'

'Sorry?'

'Pan pipes. She learned in Laos. Mr Child asked her out for a drink. I think a lot of the male teachers have made a move on her. She went along. As I said, she's in a daze. It turned out Mr Child intended a drink in the country. This involved a long drive. Not what she had expected. I suppose he had a vision of a secluded country pub but he didn't know where he was going. He *was* hopeless, you know. They went along the Great North Road in his mother's Toyota, getting further and further from town. He told her about himself – his experiences at uni and his first impressions of Lloyd-Barron Academy, his disillusion with the place. I suppose he was nervous. He just kept talking. Nesta woke up. She felt kidnapped. She said she wanted to go back. He promised to stop at the next place – a decision that brought an almost instant pay-off because round the next bend was a motel with an enormous empty car park. He swerved in. She refused to get out of the car. That's when it happened.'

Ginny is animated and quietly desperate as she tells the story. She holds her glass tightly by the stem. 'He told her how lovely she was – or something like that. Whatever it is they say. Then he picked up her hand from her lap and did this.' Ginny puts her glass down. Keeping her eyes fixed on me, she takes her left hand in her right, raises it to her mouth and runs the tip of her tongue along it from wrist to fingertip.

'Oh, no.'

'To be fair, it probably wasn't as blatant as that. But she felt his tongue.' Ginny shuddered. 'He caught a group of colleagues acting out what Nesta Robartes claimed he had done to her in private. They were wetting themselves with hilarity.'

'Until they saw him.'

Ginny nods. She puts on an expression of gleeful shock and erases it in an instant.

'I'll go and get some more drinks.' I stand up.

Ginny protests that it is her turn and begins to scrabble in her bag with the hand that a moment before crossed a threshold between one life and another, like a puppet. I had not expected so much drama from her. I gesture to her to put her purse away and walk over to the bar. The story – whatever kind of story it was – formed and set too quickly. I can't bear it.

There are several people queuing at the bar. I fail to push forward. Upturned glasses glint in the vast dresser behind the counter; a piece of polished Victoriana that is part domestic, part monumental and incorporates a large clock that looms above, marking the time. The orderliness of the backdrop contrasts with the haphazard movement around me, as people shift and jostle for position. Snatches of conversation make no sense. I am conscious of big fleshy hands that reach over the bar counter, jiggle in a pocket, or proffer a tenner. They bear some relation to Ginny's small hand, or Nesta's, or the multiplicity of hands that mocked Alan Child.

'This lady's next,' I hear a voice say.

A man in a navy blazer is speaking about me.

'Thank you,' I say.

He sports an artfully crinkled handkerchief in his top pocket and what appear to be medals on a lapel. I order two large glasses of house Merlot and a packet of dry-roasted peanuts.

'In a dream, were we?'

'Yes, must have been.'

He laughs and the laugh goes on too long; in and out, like wheezy bellows. I pay the barman, shove my bag up onto my shoulder and grasp the glasses.

'Need a hand?'

'No, thanks.'

'Chinese, is she, your friend? I was in Shanghai soon after—' I hear him say, as I retreat.

I do not know Ginny well. There are people who go back a long way; the connection through our children. I am perplexed to see her, sitting neatly in the corner of the saloon bar of The Albert, waiting for my return. Dreams insinuate our familiars in odd places – and reality is the same.

'You found an admirer. Would you like me to leave?' Ginny says, as I put the glasses down.

'I think it's you he's interested in. He asked about you.'

'Your hair looks nice, Lorna.'

'Thanks. I let it get too long.'

'It's not true that we become invisible. There's always some disgusting old creep who recognises our beauty.'

We laugh. I trust her. We have more in common than I would have guessed. Ginny and I both understand that we can't keep pounding away at the topic of Alan Child and keep any vestige of decorum. If she had been Liz Savaris, or Randal, in his day, I would have gone for a battery of questions. Ginny and I move on to more practical matters. We carry on drinking so nothing is really clear and when it is time to go – which we decide at the same moment as we remember Grace and Ross – we get unsteadily to our feet and hold onto each other's arms, either Ginny supporting me, or I her – she a good deal shorter than me and probably less inured to alcohol – as we make our way to the exit.

37

During my lunch break the following day, I receive a call from Tony Goode. He says something serious has happened: Ross has been removed from his classes as a disciplinary measure. He wants me to go to school as soon as possible but by four o'clock at the latest. He and Mr Milner will see me and a police officer might be present. I ask if Ross is all right. He repeats that it is a disciplinary matter and nothing is wrong with the physical health of the boy.

I tell him that I will set off immediately. In daylight, at one-thirty, I am aware of retracing my steps in a way that I am unconscious of at my normal time of leaving. Take the Tube at St James's Park station, change at Victoria, on to Finsbury Park; the homeward journey comes to life.

I emerge at Finsbury Park overground station with its multiple platforms. Trains hurtle through at high speed or chug to a stop. One is a streak of blended colour, the other naive in its visibility, like a child's painting. The two types of locomotion, so disturbingly different that they cannot be resolved, create a peculiar loneliness. A simple up-and-down line does not produce this desolation, nor the chaotic order of a terminus. I stand on this station every evening. Crosswinds whip the platforms and solitary people stand, not waiting but enduring.

I board an almost empty train. I sit very still, like a propped-up corpse, and wonder what ordeal is in store. The familiar stations on the line are a series of potential stopping-off points and have an allure, almost a black romance, as if I were travelling from, say, Derry to Coleraine; a journey I once went on with Randal in order to attend his grandfather's funeral. Although there is no River Foyle to be glimpsed from the window, the places outside, Hornsey or Bowes Park, possess worth that I previously failed to register and are inhabited by real people who go about their lives obliviously, or, like myself, in a state of acute anxiety. I have missed the opportunity to see these places in a right frame of mind; to look at the tin tabernacle at Bowes Park, or the old public wash house in Hornsey High Street, both of which are derelict and could fall down at any time. I shall never wander round these districts aimlessly unless the current crisis is resolved quickly and happily which seems unlikely, just as I have never explored the Mussenden Temple, County Londonderry, that was built as a library and modelled on the Temple of Vesta in Tivoli. It sits on a cliff. The train passes through a tunnel directly underneath and unless you get out at Castlerock, which we were unable to do because of Kenneth Doig's funeral, you have the tantalising knowledge that it is directly above your head but invisible. Randal insisted that I go with him which surprised me as we had not been together long. It was only when I got to know him better that I gathered that Randal would do anything to escape travelling with his parents and his brother, Michael, as a family group, and that what he dreaded above all was making an entrance with them. Aged twenty-five, I took a romantic view of his insistence and of the funeral, never having been to one, and was unprepared for the intense curiosity of his wider family. They put me down as quiet, I later discovered; a reputation that I was unable to shift since, by some fluke, we attended two more Doig funerals in the space of eighteen months: that of Randal's Uncle Frank, and of his grandmother, though Frank's was in Bootle. Being young and in love, I was unable to express the varied range of my personality at a Roman Catholic requiem mass followed by compulsory carbohydrate and alcohol intake accompanied by harp. I came across as less than animated though I was astonished to see the very same harpist in Bootle as had played in Coleraine; a red-haired woman who slightly resembled the novelist Edna O'Brien. I can only imagine that, years later, hearing the news of Randal's divorce and remarriage, his relatives – those still alive – were unsurprised. Ambitious young Randal should never have married a mouse.

At Palmers Green station there is no sign of a taxi. I consider phoning for a minicab but recall the smell of stale tobacco, the dangly toys and the sometimes deeply disturbing conversation with the driver. I dismiss the idea. I need to be in robust health to tolerate minicabs, gaiety intact. Instead, I catch a bus from Green Lanes and get off at the roundabout. I could then wait for the single-decker that serves a loopy route through suburban streets but I walk the last half-mile. I am glad of fresh air.

38

In all my sons' years at Lloyd-Barron Academy, formerly Mountwood School, I have never had to make an unscheduled visit. When Oliver broke his arm playing football and, on another occasion, ran full tilt into a glass door, I went straight to Accident and Emergency at North Middlesex University Hospital. I received innumerable letters, later emails, that outlined various misdemeanours: repeated failures to bring appropriate equipment (a towel for swimming: Ewan), subversions of the uniform (no house-colours tie, non-regulation jogging bottoms, a hat that he refused to remove indoors on the grounds that he had an unsightly head wound: Ross). There were other more esoteric communications. I was reminded that asthma inhalers should be deposited with the school nurse (Oliver) and that requests for leave of absence for religious obser-vance should be made at least one month in advance (Ross). I was also informed that my daughter's jewellery had been confiscated: a slip-up that tended to confirm my sons' excuses that the inhaler and the day off for Yom Kippur were cases of mistaken identity.

The main door to the school is locked. I ring the bell, give my name and an unseen person buzzes me in. The lobby refurbishment is complete. The area is now a large, open-plan space and resembles the entrance hall of the headquarters of a small public limited company. No trace of the receptionists' room remains. A sleek, backlit photograph about eight foot square dominates one grey-painted wall. I approach the desk, now with hardwood trim and flanked by glass panels etched with the letters L and B. The woman behind, Cathy, asks me to sign my name. She writes out a badge and hands it to me. 'They're all in the IT suite. The head's room's being decorated.'

I stare at the life-size photograph. A group of students, neatly dressed in the black-and-white Lloyd-Barron uniform are out of doors in sunshine that glows like clear acacia honey. To one side a willow tree; to the other, the edge of what appears to be a free-standing neo-classical column. Two girls sit on a bench, laptops open on their knees. Three boys, all carrying briefcases, are in light discussion with one another. I cannot imagine what was said or done to the boys to get them to behave like that. 'Pretend you are middle managers at a conference, observed by the bigwigs and with bonus time looming.' Some such instruction, combined with a morning of method acting.

'You know where to go, don't you, Mrs Parry? Left

out of here and then up the stairs. You're nice and early. Wait outside till you're called, if the door's shut.' I feel grateful to Cathy for her cheerfulness.

'They've been spending money,' I say.

Cathy rolls her eyes. 'Same old wages, my love, and longer hours. I haven't had an upgrade.'

I set off. The lighting is new but the heat is familiar. The springy carpet flows from the lobby into the corridor. I keep walking. I go through two sets of fire doors. I take off my mac. At a certain point I become aware of the sound of my heels and notice worn grey lino under my feet. I see nobody but suddenly the place is alive with muffled uproar. The walls hum with sounds of classroom strife. Without meaning to, I have strayed into a different building. I turn round, hoping to retrace my steps – more walking, more opening of fire doors. I go up a flight of stairs and find myself on an internal bridge that links two blocks together – maybe Grebe to Shearwater – and resembles the approach to a satellite terminal in a run-down part of an airport, though I am the only passenger. I check the time and pull off my jumper. As I emerge, I see that I have stopped next to a door. An ordinary, flush door, painted off-white, with a chrome latch handle. Security tape in black-and-yellow diagonal stripes is stretched across the frame in two directions, in the shape of a saltire.

'What are you doing here?'

I turn round. A man is walking towards me. He wears a charcoal-grey suit and his head is as bald as an egg.

I am unable to speak, not because of the man with his attitude of banal menace, but because of the door. I cannot take my eyes off it.

'Lorna Parry,' I manage to say. 'A mother. I have an appointment with the head. I am looking for the IT suite. I got lost. Perhaps you can redirect me.'

I straighten my shirt.

'ID?' The man squares up in front of me.

'Sorry?'

'You should have been given a badge.'

I touch my shirt and, finding nothing there, fumble in the folds of the mac I have taken off. It takes me a few seconds to locate the piece of plastic in a pocket.

He steps aside, lowers his chin and speaks into the hands-free microphone that is clipped to his lapel. Behind him is the door, criss-crossed with tape. It is a piece of wood, circa 1960, encrusted with layers of paint and burdened with an emotion I am unable to name. It is full of un-meaning. I hear the words 'woman' and 'alleged parent', then the fuzzy sound of a reply.

The man raises his head and reapproaches. He fingers the badge and glances at my face.

'Which way should I go?'

'Put it on.'

'Sorry?'

'The badge. Put it on. ID must be visible at all times.'

I slip my arms into the mac and fix on the badge.

'Follow me,' he says.

39

PC Sally Reynolds's hair is pinned up under her hat. She is young. I am glad she is here. She says that she is the school's liaison police officer and that Ross probably recognises her because she marked and registered his bike. She is involved on this occasion because malicious communication is a crime. Under Section 1 of The Malicious Communications Act 1998, it is an offence to send an indecent, offensive or threatening letter, electronic communication or other article to another person.

The IT suite is a narrow, low-ceilinged room, lit by long fluorescent tubes that emit pinkish light. There are four windows that look directly onto a building a few metres away. Salt stains run down the brickwork in uneven lines, like chalk half-rubbed out on a blackboard. The computers are covered and the tables on which they stand have been crammed together to make room for the head's temporary office. Furniture – presumably brought up from downstairs – has been arranged as in a three-sided box. A filing cabinet, an indoor plant on a plinth, an upended trunk, a coat stand, two fireside chairs covered in blue Dralon, a low table, a group of stacked cardboard packing cases on which stand an electric kettle, a coffee-making machine and several mugs and canisters – all these are placed in what I imagine is a simulacrum of the place the head has been ejected from – a home-from-home that I find almost touching.

While PC Sally Reynolds is talking in her friendly, sensible voice, the door opens. I hear a creak but I do not turn round. The person who has come in moves slowly down the room, possibly on tiptoe as the footfall is irregular and faint. The head, Tony Goode, seated in a black faux-leather executive chair behind a slab of a desk, gives no indication that he has noticed this person and even when Mary de Silva draws close, picks up one of the classroom chairs, carries it to a spot next to Mr Milner and sits down on it, fails to acknowledge her. She joins our semicircle: Mr Milner, PC Sally Reynolds, Ross and me. Our backs are turned to a notional audience. Amrita, the head's secretary, to one side of the desk, takes notes.

'Sorree,' Mary de Silva mouths as she scrapes her chair into position.

'I'm done for the moment,' PC Sally Reynolds says.

Mr Milner, in his red tie and non-matching red shirt,

repositions himself so that he can see all of us. With a skill that comes from professional experience, he makes eye contact with everyone present and holds our attention with a rolling programme of regard. He speaks of the seriousness of causing offence or needless anxiety to innocent persons, disseminating false information and bringing the academy into disrepute. He says that in line with safeguarding procedures and the Lloyd-Barron Academy behaviour policy that we all signed up to and are well aware of, no comments should be made with reference to the academy, its staff, governors, students, families or any associated persons on social networking sites. He says that some people consider social networking sites to be like chatting with mates but they are not like chatting with mates. They are highly visible and anyone putting stuff out there should ask themselves whether they want what they are putting out to be on prime-time television. Furthermore, and setting the issue of social media to one side, the fact remains that, had he overheard any student so much as whispering such cowardly and disrespectful claptrap as Ross saw fit to spread about, he would have hauled him in immediately and given him a good talking-to that he wouldn't have forgotten in a hurry. 'Have you anything to say?' he asks Ross.

Ross, who has been staring at a space on the floor between his feet says, 'No, sir.' He keeps his head bowed.

'Do you realise the seriousness of this matter?'

'Yes, sir.'

'And what do you have to say about it?'

'Sorry, sir.'

'Sorry to whom?'

'To everyone relevant, sir.'

'Such as?'

'The school?'

'The academy,' Tony Goode chips in.

Mr Milner nods in acknowledgement and continues. 'What about Mr Child? You set about destroying the reputation of someone who, in this tragic situation, can't answer back.'

'Yes, sir. I'm sorry.'

'What about Mr Child's family?'

'They don't know, sir.'

'We sincerely hope they don't. But they might. They *still* might.'

'Do you want me to say sorry to them, sir?'

'No, Ross. There's no need to cause them unnecessary pain. They have enough on their plate.' Mr Milner pauses. 'Do you have an explanation for what you did?'

'No, sir.'

'This was premeditated and planned. It wasn't a brainstorm. There were photographs. A series of them.' Mr Milner takes his eyes off Ross and looks at me. 'They

185

were, in themselves, innocuous – though why anyone wastes their time recording such things beats me. No, it was the clever-Dick, smutty captions our friend here added, that turned a childish game into a potentially criminal act.' He turned back to Ross. 'What went through your skull?'

Ross is silent.

'I asked you a question.'

'Nothing, sir.'

'Was anyone else involved?'

'No, sir.'

'You did this entirely alone?'

'Yes, sir.'

Mr Milner turns to me. 'This is the trouble. Ross won't tell us anything. He doesn't assist us. The only thing in his favour is that he has admitted to it.'

'Under pressure. He came under pressure. I addressed the entire upper school. As a body. Leadership in action.' Tony Goode uses his whole jaw when he speaks, as if chewing a chunk of meat.

I clear my throat. 'I'd find it helpful to know exactly what Ross is supposed to have done.'

'Doig did it. He came clean,' Mr Goode says.

'All right. I withdraw the "supposed". What did he do?'

Tony Goode presses the heels of his hands against the edge of the desk and pushes back. The reclining

186

mechanism of the chair moves faster or further than he expects. For an instant he struggles, then with a jolt and an intake of breath, he rights himself.

'I'll have a drink please, Amrita.' He shoves his shirt back into the top of his trousers.

'Water?'

'Yes, water. Of course, water. There's dust every-where. The sooner this refurbishment lark's over the better.' He presses his hands together, palm on palm, and touches his lips. 'Mother. You asked a question. I'm not going to answer it. Ask your son later and don't expect to be thrilled by the reply. I have forgotten the pacific minutiae and everyone else present has forgotten the pacific minutiae and that's where it shall remain. Buried. What are you scrabbling around for, Amrita?'

'I'm trying to find a water glass, Mr Goode.'

'Any kind of glass'll do. I'm not fussed.'

Amrita is kneeling in front of the upended trunk. Its lid is ajar and functions as a door. Sally Reynolds is observing the trunk. Like me, she will notice that it stands on little wheels and that the interior is crammed with bottles.

'Let's move on. We've all got better things to do. I have, anyway. What action are we going to take with Rob Doig? I'll tell you. For starters, a fixed-term exclusion. Five school days, commencing Monday. This will be a punishment and a warning to the others and it will give Mr Milner and PC Rendell time to make further investigations. We have seized and confiscated his phone. Thank you, Amrita.' Tony Goode has been addressing the fourth wall but breaks off to take a gulp of water from the balloon-shaped brandy glass she has placed on the desk. 'Five days for Rob Doig to remove the offensive material. He will use his wit and wisdom to undertake this. And don't tell me it's impossible. What goes up can come down. Do aircraft fly for ever? They do not. They need to refuel, as we all do. Five days for Robert to make a full written apology, in writing to me, personally. That's not getting off lightly. Fixed-term exclusion can turn into permanent exclusion. On my say-so. Are we in agreement? Mr Milner, PC Rendell?'

Mary de Silva raises her hand in a queenly wave.

'What are you doing here?' Tony Goode stares at her.

'Mr Goode. I'm the responsible adult.'

'What's that when it's at home? No, don't tell me. Do you have a vote?'

'I believe so.'

'I don't. We'll argue about it later. We don't need you. It's unanimous. Passed *non quem*. Rob, I'm sick of the

188

sight of you. Go home with your mother. Mother, I'll revert back to you.'

'To me? Really?' I say.

Ross kicks my ankle.

'To you,' the head affirms.

40

As we walk back through the car park, Ross vomits. I put a hand on his back and give him a clutch of tissues when it is over.

'Where's the car?' he says.

'I don't have the car. I came straight from work. We'll catch the little bus. It won't take long.'

'I don't want to catch the little bus.'

'Well, we can walk, I suppose. Why not?'

'Can't you go and fetch the car?'

'Yes, I could do but that seems quite a complicated thing. No one will be on the bus, Ross, at this time of day. You won't meet anyone.' I look into his face. 'Where will you wait?'

'You get the little bus and I'll start walking. You'll see me.'

'That's not entirely helpful. I tend to look at the road.'

'OK.'

'I can't stop for you on the mini-roundabout or on Green Lanes. It's a red route.'

'Cool. See you.'

He sets off and I stay at the bus stop. I watch him until he reaches the first curving bend of the road and disappears out of sight. I see him again from the bus about ten minutes later through smeary fingerprints on glass. He is about halfway along the interminable street. Trees are coming into leaf and there are splashes of yellow and blue in some of the front gardens: early daffodils and scillas, maybe, or grape hyacinths. I am unable to tell from the moving bus.

I have no trouble finding him. Ross was right. The black school blazer. The reddish fair hair. Scarcely anyone else is out and about. The pavements are deserted. Collecting the car is exactly the type of indulgence that Randal disapproves of but kindness is often a slow and illogical way of getting from A to B. What mothers can do to help is limited. It becomes clear after a number of years that, in spite of its basis in animal biology, the process of bringing up children is itself an immensely long detour and one that is likely to last right up until the moment of death. I wave when I see Ross and drive on to a point where I can safely execute a U-turn. I stop the car beside him, lean over and open the passenger door because the automatic unlock has stopped working. He gets in and dumps his bag at his feet. It takes up as much space as a large, sitting dog.

'If you've forgotten anything, I'm sure Jude can bring it round,' I say.

We wait at traffic lights. 'She does the same subjects as you, she'll be able to give you her notes. She owes you one.'

He does not respond.

'She took the photos, didn't she? What were these captions? Tell me.' I glance at his face. He gives nothing away. 'I hope she appreciates this,' I say in my most sarcastic voice.

We set off again.

'Stop the car, Mum.' Ross opens the passenger door while we are still moving across the junction. I scream at him. We get to the other side. The van driver behind me leans on his hooter, as I pull in to the kerb without warning.

Ross, hanging out of the car door, retches, then swivels back into the passenger seat.

'OK?'

'Nothing came up.'

'We'll go then?'

He nods.

'Shut the door and put your seat belt back on.'

We need to get home. Distraction was the tactic I used when the boys were carsick. Songs, I-Spy. They were little.

'That illuminated picture in reception. I wanted to ask—'

'What illuminated picture?' he says grudgingly.

'In reception.'

'I never go to reception. Sorry. Went. I never went to reception.'

'Let's wait and see, shall we? Anyway, in this photo – which is a kind of Paradise scene, as it were Princeton comes to N13 – there is a willow. A weeping willow. And a column. I've never seen either – or anywhere remotely similar in the school grounds. I mean, is there some carefully tended secret garden kept specifically, or pacifically, as we've learned to say, for advertising purposes? Somewhere they can choreograph a collection of the best-looking pupils, of varied skin colour, tell them to smile and say "Specialising in Success" or some other specious phrase? They aren't real. They look like, I don't know, embryonic alumni. Do they even come from Lloyd-Barron Academy? Maybe they were snatched from their mothers at birth and brought up in a hall of mirrors to speak in sentences that have no subject or main verb, later to be hired out as eye fodder for school brochures. Schools are actually full of decent people who do a good job. Why should they have to sell themselves, as though they are a brand of toothpaste? Every service is commodified. Where's the learning? Where's the love? One day, they'll wake up and find—' I suddenly hear myself shrieking and stop.

There is an uncanny silence inside the car. Outside, traffic passes on the opposite carriageway. The bus ahead wheezes to a stop. I brake and wait while passengers get on and off. A woman bumps a twin buggy from bus platform to kerb. Scaffolding is going up on a nearby building. Metal tubes clang and clink. Men shout as they work. What are those mans doing? Ross used to say, up to the age of three, though his language was mostly accurate. A coupler falls to the ground. I glance at Ross. His head is turned away. His hands lie still on his lap; an empty space where his phone used to be.

41

I must have rehearsed what I would say if my father ever suggested that Jane Brims might join us for Sunday lunch because the moment he does so I have a faint memory of ripostes that are far from fit for purpose. My reply is neither trenchant, as per the mental rehearsals, nor gracious, nor kind. 'Sunday week? There's a lot going on, Dad. Oh God. Oh, OK. The more the merrier, I suppose.'

His slight but detectable embarrassment in the context of the day's events strikes me as paltry. How absurd to have minor emotions. I have to stop myself from telling him to leave me alone.

I put the handset down. I am shaking. I close my eyes and try to calm myself. My father will be sitting, glum, in his chair. He will turn on the radio and hope for trumpets. My hands pick up the phone again and I call Liz.

'I don't believe she's one of my mother's cousins. She targeted him. She reads the obits and then shows up at funerals waving bogus pieces of paper. And Dad fell for it – the innocent. Do you know what else? God, I can't believe this, Liz. She made him go to *Sweeney Todd* the other afternoon.' I am on a strange kind of high, not far off hysteria. I hear the strain in my voice.

'That's OK. If they can put up with being surrounded by kids texting and eating, good for them. They are elderly, Lorna.'

'I'm not complaining about the time of day – though, I agree, matinees are hell. A West End musical? He's never been to one in his life. I mean, it's so remote from his usual fare of television sport and Radio Three. And Jane's not truly elderly. She would shudder to hear you say the word. I told you, didn't I, she's younger than Dad? She still thinks of herself as peachy. She sort of preens. If we were on Skype I could show you.' I begin to do the legs business – Jane's sock-revealing cabaret. My mouth is small and simpering.

'I get the picture. Not too attractive. Don't make a habit of it, Lorna. The wind might change.'

I feel ill imitating Jane Brims. 'And another thing. When I said, "Gory!" – about *Sweeney Todd* – Dad said in the mildest voice without a hint of apology, "Jane likes Steven Sondheim."'

'Fair enough,' Liz says. 'It's not a crime.'

'But he didn't add, "apparently". That shocked me.'

'I think he must sense your hostility. I can feel it now,' Liz says.

'If you spend all your life being gently ironic and suddenly that goes . . . I have this picture of him with his bony knees pressed into the seat in front, clinging to the overcoat folded on his lap, as he swooshes down the rake of the upper circle in some nightmare funfair ride.'

'It's possible he's harboured a secret love of musicals all this time and suppressed it because of your mother. She was very clear about her likes and dislikes. I felt completely crushed when I told her that my favourite novel was *Jonathan Livingstone Seagull*.'

'She hadn't heard of it.'

'Exactly. She was right too! It was utter rubbish. Don't get obsessed with this Jane woman. She's not important.'

'What shall I give her to eat though, Liz? My mind's gone blank.'

'Does she have special dietary requirements?'

'I don't think so. Dad would have said, wouldn't he?'

'You'd better ask. If she's not allergic to nuts, you could make the seared salmon with pistachio crust you told me about. I made it the other day. It's dead simple. If you don't have any Thai fish sauce in your larder, just use good old Worcestershire.'

'I'm touched that you think I have a larder, Liz. You obviously don't remember my kitchen. Not sure about the salmon thing. I mean, even though you say it's not effortful it will look as if I've been trying. I suppose I could just tip it onto the plates, kind of upside down, so that it bears no resemblance to a cookery photo.'

'Plonk a bottle labelled "Poison" on the table, why don't you? You may be grateful one day that William has someone to take care of him. Pull out the long curly bits from his eyebrows – and far worse, as the years go by. Change his nappies. It will take the burden from you. Your brother won't be any bloody use, will he?'

I am shocked that Liz has deposited Jane in The Heronry as if the deal were done. I take a few moments to recover. 'You're right. Hugh will be hopeless but it won't come to that. I expect Dad will peg out. Women rot slowly and men drop down dead. Mum was an exception. I'll get left looking after Jane Brims! It's because men go through a testosterone storm in adolescence. The memory of it kills them like a thunderbolt.'

'Lorna, that is so unscientific. Their hormones make them drive too fast or stab each other. They die then and there in their late teens or early twenties and affect the statistics. It has no bearing on the way they age. How are your testosterone-fuelled lot?'

'Thank you. They're well.'

'Ewan?'

'Nothing new.'

There is more give in Liz than is sometimes the case. I wonder whether to tell her about Ross. Liz can be severe. She never flinches from attacking me on the subject of Ewan. At some level, she grasps the nub of the matter. My spinelessness. Ewan's spinelessness. In the department of philology and applied linguistics at Aberystwyth University, they must hold meetings at which it is decided that certain procedures are fruitless and should be discontinued. What these might be, I have no idea because, although I ask, the place and its workings are a mystery to me. Liz will be the leading light of such meetings and cut through the crap and tell them in no uncertain terms to change their ways. They will mosey back to their desks, or scurry – I really do not know how they behave there – and it will all be new for about five minutes.

'Well, you know what I think,' Liz says.

'Yes, I do,' I say.

'All this pairing that's going on . . . how does that affect you?'

'Cutbacks at work? Thank you for asking. It's a disaster. I'm running the place on a shoestring.'

'What are you talking about, Lorna?'

'What are *you* talking about? The recession? The chancellor says we're out of it.'

'I'm lost. You do have a tendency to divert a personal question. I was thinking of William and Ross both at it like rabbits, one presumes. Richard Watson, is he in the picture?'

'Like rabbits? Oh God. Don't let's go there. No. No, I told you before.'

There is a brief pause. Liz suspects something which in one sense is a fair response as I see Richard most weeks now. She is, however, wrong about the picture. Mine, an amateur daub, is now overprinted with Judge Jeffrey's courtroom. I am answering the question that lies behind the question. Take into consideration the frame or the mount. No, avoid the word 'mount'.

'You should find yourself a man. A proper one this time.'

'Oh, a proper one? Yes, of course, I must ask around.'

'Libby's come in,' she says.

I begin peeling potatoes and cannot stop. The repetitive strokes of the peeler, the digging out of eyes, the clean reveal – I am in the flow and end up preparing enough food for a family of six. Jude does not turn up at the usual time. Seven, seven-thirty, eight, nine. She does not turn up.

42

The weekend is like a pressure headache that goes on and on. There is nothing to take and no relief. Every few hours, I look in on Ross who remains in his room. He is in bed or he is crouching on the floor, playing a game on his old Xbox. I try to get him to talk but he is as terse as he was in the IT suite. I detect both stoicism and recklessness in the front he presents. His sole contribution is to ask if I am going to tell his dad. I say that it is his choice. I won't mention anything if he doesn't want me to. 'Same applies to Grandad,' I say. 'He doesn't need to know anything at this stage, does he?'

'What do you mean, at this stage?' Ross says.

'Your five days of exclusion.'

'That's not what you meant. You think there's going to be a next stage.'

There is a strong smell of boy in the unventilated bedroom.

I go on up to Ewan. I tell him what has happened to Ross. 'Be nice to him,' I say. 'You're both at home. It's an opportunity for brotherly love in action. A little rapprochement is in order. Have a word. Try to find out what he's done.'

Ewan sits at his desk. He half-turns his head and nods.

'Ewan? Please say something.'

'What a mess. I'm sorry,' he says.

'Thank you,' I say. 'Thank you for speaking to me.'

On the commute into London on Monday morning, a new light-headedness distances me from delays to the First Capital Connect train service. I stand on the platform at Palmers Green station, cold but strangely unconcerned. Noise is hyper-loud. The interminable train announcements, telephones breaking into snatches of tunes and recorded animal noises open into echo chambers of pain. It is a relief to get to the office and sit at my desk.

I repeatedly call the landline at home. No one picks up. I try Ewan's mobile and get his voice-messaging service. I send him texts but nothing comes back. I do not know how they are spending the day, Ewan and Ross. I am at work.

In the middle of the morning, Lloyd-Barron Academy sends me a message with the subject heading, '*Choices and Destinations*'; words that last week I would have taken for meaningless flannel. I break into a cold sweat and imagine a 'managed move' to a pupil referral centre. I know the jargon, having tracked all possible outcomes, late into the night.

Throughout their studentship but notably from Year 10 the students at Lloyd-Barron Academy are strongly encouraged to consider their strengths and capabilities and potential future careers. Are you able to raise aspirations by participating in their Speaker Programme? Notable speakers in the past have included lawyers, sportsmen, web designers and politicians. Further information at http://www. Lloyd-BarronAcademy.org/cobbling-rubbish-together/#sthash.p973000.16to24yearoldsunemployed

At lunch-time, I walk to St James's Park and sit on a bench by the lake. I have a low tolerance for squirrel worship but today the delight on people's faces as they spot a tail a few metres away strikes me as wholly innocent. A child squeals, *'Mama! Guarda! Uno scoiattolo!'* – or in some other language – and the family group stands rapt, gazing at the small grey animal that sits upright with its stomach exposed and its front paws pendant. The watchers, unfamiliar with London squirrels, are hushed, hardly daring to move, unaware, having just entered the park, that the creature is one of many and lost to wildness – nerveless as a gull or an urban pigeon, and capable of shinning up a trouser leg.

On the far side of the water, a pink umbrella held high like a flag precedes a squad of tourists in flapping, clear plastic capes. The bridge is thronged with people who take photographs with phones and cameras. Buckingham Palace one way; fairy-tale turrets of Whitehall the other. I hear a thrum of traffic at my back. The two tiny lake islands, West and Duck, screened by willows and reeds, are nesting havens. There are also notional islands on firm land, green areas of tranquillity, in sight of visitors but not disturbed by them. They shift from hour to hour, minute to minute, like a moving map. Waterfowl walk about on the grass and grub for worms. I call Ginny.

'Yes, Grace mentioned the exclusion,' she says.

'Tony Goode said he would get back – correction – "revert" to me. He might make an example of Ross so that it never happens again – or he might be lenient. It's all a stupid, hideous mess – though I still don't know precisely what—' I break off.

A brief pause. 'The disclosure of where, precisely, Mr Child's death took place is causing massive problems.' Her parents' rep voice. 'That more than the supposed contents of his rucksack – suspender belt, fishnet stockings, plastic bag, I think it was – and the assertion that at least he would die happy if it all went wrong.'

'Oh God. Ross didn't say that, did he?' My heart thuds under my coat.

'Students flocked to look at the door. The door,' Ginny repeats as though I am deaf. 'It seems Mr Child was in the habit of using the cupboard to change into his cycling gear. It's a pity it wasn't kept locked. He went off on his bike in the lunch hour. I told you he stopped going into the staffroom, didn't I?'

I say yes, though it pains me to speak.

'They are leaving bunches of flowers and soft toys. They stick up Post-it notes. Senior management closed the corridor but this had the unintended consequence of cutting off four classrooms on the first floor of Shearwater. Children piled up behind the barrier of tape. Heaven knows who put it up. It was like a cat's cradle. The kids screamed. Someone yelled, "Fire!" When Mrs Anstey got scissors to the tape and let them past they stampeded through the old building and flung themselves down the stairs. A girl in Year Eight fell and broke her wrist.'

'So the whole school believes that Mr Child died in a sex game that went wrong. There might be copycat experiments.'

'Oh, you are so funny, Lorna. They're all doing it, anyway. The window ropes! They come close to hanging themselves on a daily basis. A thrill is a thrill, you know. No, the students saw the photos and worked out what truly happened. They aren't interested in words and many of them are wilfully illiterate.'

'The cupboard as a must-see destination. I had no idea. I'm so sorry.'

I am struck that I need not be having this conversation. I was calm enough watching the ducks. There is often something wrong with an out-of-doors phone call. The scene is broad and in motion. Wind blows through the trees. Drizzle pits holes in the water. Birds take off and land. On West Island, a tree surgeon found the remains of a man, together with vodka bottles and a yellow cushion. His identity, discerned from a passport, was that of a sixty-nine-year-old American, Robert Moore, known to the police as an obsessive who sent hundreds of packages and letters to the Queen. The letters were of extraordinary length, up to 600 pages, and some of the packages contained obscene photographs.

'The fuss will die down,' Ginny says. 'They just have to wait. I'll ask Grace to find out whether the security guard is patrolling. They might have dismissed him already. What I can't understand is why Ross admitted to doing it. He used a false address – the school would never have traced him.'

I am on the point of explaining that Ross has taken sole responsibility for what was likely to have been a joint offence with Jude Bennet-Neerhoff when Ginny continues. 'Of course, if he hadn't admitted it, the others might have grassed him up. They are against grassing up but they have a strong sense of respect. For their nans, for the armed forces and for the dead. Ross might have chosen to get in first. Grace showed me. She said she thought the pictures and comments had been up there a while. She's not really into social media. I was disgusted, actually.'

'So they were in circulation before he died? Alan Child *saw* them?'

'I can't say one way or the other, Lorna.'

The phone slips from my gloved hand onto the bench beside me with a thud. A tinny voice speaks from it; pauses and speaks again. I pick it up.

'. . . always complex reasons, Lorna, and there would have been a predisposition . . .'

I can't listen to this. I need reassurance on one point only. I cut across Ginny's balanced explanations. 'The photos were news to Mr Milner and Mr Goode. They'd only just seen them. So maybe none of the teachers—'

'Senior management are slow on the uptake. They'd be the last to know, wouldn't they?'

43

As I pass a bin, I discard the uneaten lunch-time snack that I hastily assembled at seven o'clock in the morning. It is still intact in its aluminium-foil wrapper. I head towards Queen Anne's Gate. Recently planted bedding plants, banked and ranked, all face the same way like a choir. The pedestrian crossing signal on Birdcage Walk beeps. Taxis come to a halt. Ahead, to one side of the path by the drinking fountain, a couple, a man and a woman, bend over a small child. The adults are tall, well dressed, both wearing trench coats over steam-pressed linen. Their smartness, unusual for casual strollers in the park, catches my eye. Once or twice, I have encountered wedding parties – shafts of colour against the green, a swirl of white – but there is no sign of a wedding. These people are on their own, hanging out by the water fountain that no longer functions. The seated boy was vandalised some years ago and now has a new white head and a line around his neck. He sits on his marble plinth and presides over dry basins and gasping fish.

The woman balances elegantly, in a practised way, on

high heels. She hovers over the child, seemingly reasoning with him, or explaining, though he is below the age of reason; less than two years old. He holds a paper bag by one corner in a closed fist. He retains it through inertia and shows no interest in it, or in the contents. It seems that he might at any moment let go. This is a concern for the woman. She leans further forward and places her hand over the child's. Neither her action nor what she says makes any impression on him.

The man gestures at the little boy to get his attention. He points at the sky, then raises and lowers his arms a few times. The woman puts her free hand in the paper bag and, withdrawing it, makes a scattering motion. The child, up too close to the dumb show to see a meaning, continues to ignore them, obstinate or lost in a world of his own. Exasperated, the woman dips again and flings a handful of crumbs around the boy's feet. As two or three pigeons fly in low, she upends the bag and steps to one side. The man takes a backward stride. He raises his camera. Within seconds, the boy is surrounded. He bursts into wild, loud crying, puts up his hands and covers his face. The camera clicks repeatedly. Pigeon life engulfs him, convulsive movements of flapping wings and bobbing heads; they heave like the contents of an exposed gut. The child is rigid with terror. He ventures a look through splayed fingers, then stretches out his arms and tries to run forward.

'No, Benny. Stay,' the woman calls. 'It's fun.'

The man keeps clicking. 'Hey, stop him crying, Rena.'

'Don't cry, honey.'

I draw level. 'He'll hate you,' I say – quite loudly. They are not expecting to hear from me.

'Pardon me?' the woman says.

'Your son will hate you.'

'Oh my God, Carl, did you hear that? This woman is some kind of witch.' The mother sweeps forward and gathers up her wailing child. 'It's OK, Benny, it's OK. This lady is not a nice person but she is going to walk away and we are never, ever going to see her again.'

'Leave it, Rena,' the man says. 'Maybe the woman is sick.'

I keep walking. I leave the park. The crossing signal is red for pedestrians but I step off the pavement. '*Achtung!*' I hear from a warning voice behind me. A lull in the traffic enables me to reach the opposite pavement unharmed. I go along Queen Anne's Gate, the goods entrance to the Ministry of Justice to my right. I cross the road at Petty France by the entrance to St James's Park Tube station. People mill about, check their phone messages, top up their Oyster cards, queue for the cash machine. I plunge in among them. For a moment, I am drawn towards the ticket barrier and the lure of escape but carry on moving. In the safety of the throng I slow down a little. I walk through the arcade towards the bronze-and-glass doors of the Transport for London entrance, breathing unevenly. The smell of coffee calms me, the ordinary voices chatting on telephones. In his kiosk, the shoe mender is re-soling a shoe, trimming its edges on the abrading wheel. The high-pitched rasp, like a recording of crude dentistry, sets off memories of pain.

44

I tell Ross that I know something of the content of his malicious messages and that he should give me a proper account in his own words.

'Who told you?' he snaps back.

'That's not your business. Have you written the apology? Have you taken the photos down? I can't find them anywhere but I'm probably looking in the wrong places. Do you want to be permanently excluded? I can't believe what you've done.' I wait for a response. Then I leave the room.

Ross has all the time in the world and does nothing. He says nothing. The hours in which he might communicate with Tony Goode are fewer and the air seems thin, as if we now live at a higher altitude. I check my emails constantly. I pray that Alan Child never saw the offensive material and that I will discover conclusively that this is the case. The word 'hope' does not describe what I do. My mental exertion – backward in conjectures and forward in previsions – has earth-moving equipment behind it.

What is this stuff? Oliver asked, pointing accusingly at the piles of papers on the kitchen table that accumulated in the months after Randal departed. He had hated interrogating me. He meant not to do it because asking made the situation worse. He held out until the last possible second and then words erupted in a splutter. Is this a division of assets? He had come across the phrase but it was as alien to him as the words 'Mortgage Agreement' that appeared on the uppermost file. Whereas. Now therefore. His voice cracked with anger. I suppose the grilling was intended for Randal and concealed a different barrage of questions. Within weeks, there had been less money to go round. That shocked the boys. I kept their small allowances going but the casual handing over of the debit card for this, that and the other stopped.

To persist is not to clear up a matter. An answer can leave the questioner as much in the dark as I am at present. In these circumstances, it is as though the tricks of empathy – connecting and imagining – are subverted and made malign.

I trudge up the stairs to visit both sons. I harangue Ross and then spoil the effect by adding sentences about supper, the longer hours of daylight. I remark that next week is a new one. I can do verbal optimism, the bolstering, maternal kind though in the manner of someone who continually scrubs her hands raw, fearing violent implosion

213

if the ritual is omitted. I give him permission to buy a new phone. 'On condition you answer my texts. Do you understand?'

For months, a bunch of flowers was tied to a lamp post to commemorate a pedestrian who had died on the crossing in Grosvenor Gardens at the junction with Lower Grosvenor Place. Fresh flowers replaced the old and then the last lot turned brown in the cellophane wrapper. In other parts of London, I have seen white-painted bikes. It happened here, they seem to say, not at the crematorium or the garden of remembrance: here. I cannot square these desperate memorials with my son's casual cruelty.

45

At ten to eight on Saturday evening, the doorbell rings. Ross shoots out of his room and hurtles down the stairs. I am washing a Savoy cabbage in the sink. I undo it as though it were a huge tight-petalled rose. The front door opens and shuts. I hear nothing above the trickle of water on the leaves. Then, perhaps because of some slight movement, I sense that they – Ross and whoever is there – remain in the hall.

'Come upstairs. Why are you still standing there?'

I do not hear a reply but there are other means. We mouth and make facial expressions. I read only the other day that researchers at Ohio State University have taught computers to recognise twenty-one different human emotions from the face. Professor Martinez has more than tripled the 'palette' by combining them. Happily disgusted. Sadly angry. We don't feel just one thing at a time, the professor says. This was news, apparently.

I turn off the tap.

'What's the matter?' Ross's voice comes from the same place as before.

Loudly silent in the hall.

'Let's go for a run,' Jude says.

'You've only just arrived.'

'So?'

'It's dark.'

'We can run in the dark.'

They begin to bicker over messages sent or not sent, missed calls and so on. They are like winged insects trapped in a jar. Their words beat pointlessly.

'What's wrong with you?' Ross says.

'Nothing. I just don't want to be indoors all the time.'

'We're never indoors all the time. We'll go out tomorrow.'

'You needn't come if you don't want to.'

'You don't want me to come?'

'I do.'

'But you'll go anyway. Is that right?'

'Yes.'

'So we don't get to decide stuff together?'

'Course we do.'

'But not now this minute. You're going for a run and that's it.'

I hear a scuffle – and a chime, as one of them bumps into or kicks the boxes that stand in the hall. I no longer recall what is in there apart from the clock. I conclude, since time has passed, that I cannot want the contents.

The front door slams and they are gone. Ross, beside Jude, or ahead. I know the quiet streets with their pattern of lighted windows, dark bushes, front paths, columnar cherry trees, parked cars on tarmacked driveways. Down one, up the next, across a main road, past the park gates. Ross has an easy style of running, stolid but relaxed. One of them might be the conductor but neither is the music. The park railings go by like notes on a stave. They go on for ever. The moon is a gauzy half-circle with an ill-defined edge above the rooftops. I see it from the kitchen window.

They return just before nine-thirty. The two of them go upstairs. I hear thuds, as of objects falling over; more arguing. They come down again and into the kitchen. Their faces glow with health. I say hello. Jude sits down. Ross bypasses the table and goes over to the back door. He stands there staring out, his hands rammed into his pockets. A neighbour's newly installed security light comes on and targets the garden with a penetrating, green-tinted glare.

'Did you have a good run?' I ask.

'That white cat's just come over the fence. It's gross. Like a big furry maggot,' Ross says.

The cat knows that his movements trigger the light. His method of scaling the fence has become increasingly furtive in the nights since the device was installed. He has lost his feline abandon. Instead of leaping, he tries to clamber and slither up the wooden slats, using claws as crampons, and at the top flattens himself to the maximum which is not a lot, given that he is fat and fluffy, but perhaps, from his own point of view, feels like a meaningful effort, just as when wearing a tight skirt I engage my stomach muscles without producing an elegant outline. He crouches, bathed in the interrogatory beam, having activated the sensor, then descends with disappointed caution, giving off a palpable sense of failure.

I could make these observations out loud but my comments would not be welcome. The sound of my voice, irrespective of what I say, is a wasteful use of energy.

'Any news?' I say to Jude as I serve out reheated shepherd's pie.

'It's lifting its tail and is about to spray. Do you want it to stink out your garden?' Ross's face is pressed against the glass.

The security light goes off.

'We're going to eat now, Ross. It's late. Come and sit down,' I say.

He joins us at the table. Neither he nor Jude speaks. She reaches for the water jug. She drinks. Ross picks up his fork. Jude picks up her fork.

'What's this silence about?' I say.

Ross stands up. 'Come on, Jude, let's go upstairs.'

'No.'

'Please,' he says.

'If you make me get up, I'll go home.'

'He's having a hard time, Jude. Just be nice to him.'

'Shut the fuck up,' Ross yells – at me.

He remains standing – stranded somehow. Jude tries a mouthful of mince.

Ross jabs a finger at me. 'A drop-in death clinic wouldn't be good enough for you,' he shouts – but the high moment has passed. He sits down again. He grabs the ketchup and shakes it. With a flick of his wrist, the bottle hits the rim of his plate. It tilts, cracks and a chip of china whizzes past Jude's ear and flies across the room. She flinches but the response is purely physical. Her eyes stay the same. Her mind is elsewhere. The last tomatoey clot comes out with a glug.

46

In the middle of the night, a noise or a danger that at first seems part of a dream breaks through the barrier of sleep. I sit up. There are the shadows on the bedroom walls. The outline of the chair, its struts delineated but skewed. The two candlesticks on the chest of drawers, also distorted by the angle of dusky orange street light that comes through the curtains. I register nothing unfamiliar. A siren in the distance starts up, grows louder and fades away. The house is quiet. I slide down under the covers again.

Unable to sleep, I get up and go along to the bathroom. When I come out I hear low voices in Ross's room. There is a line of light under the door. I walk on by and return to bed. I lie there. A few minutes later, I hear footsteps and the click of Oliver's bedroom door.

Months ago, soon after Jude started to come to the house, I was woken by a deep, low groan. Another groan followed; it began quietly and expanded into a long, sensuous foghorn of sound. What the . . .? I listened. The next noise, an intemperate, military-sounding fart, disclosed, unmistakably, Ross's saxophone. I was relieved, that night, for Ewan's sake as much as my own, that we were spared audible cries of love. Now they sleep in separate rooms.

Jude told me – when she got to know me – that Crews Hill is full of garden centres. You can buy anything. Reptiles. Birds. Fake grass. No mowing, no watering, no mud, no maintenance. Child safe, pet friendly. The Windsor, the Cotswold, the Norfolk. The fake grass has names? I warmed to the girl who offered information in a sullen, slightly breathless voice. Yes. I don't know which is which. I think one is maybe a bit greener, or a bit thicker, or something. Gosh. Life is full of surprises, I said. I must make a trip to one of these garden centres. I need tulips for the tubs. What colour shall I get? Red, pink? My mother liked pink, but not any old pink. Angelique was her favourite. Jude leant forward, her expression serious. No, don't go there. The owners are evil. They won't let you go out the way you came in. Even if you see straight away that they don't have what you want, they make you go for this massive long walk, up and down the aisles and through the tills. I promise you, even if you were ill, they wouldn't let you out. *Les fleurs du mal*, I said. Thanks for the tip. So what else happens in Crews Hill? Say, round the back of the garden centres, in the off streets? Houses and bungalows, Jude

221

said. It's very quiet. My parents like it. They prefer it to being in town. We can see fields and woods from the back windows. My mum rides. There are stables at the end of our lane. In the daytime, you might get an engineer in a white van come to mend someone's boiler, or something. In the night-time, nothing. Eerie, but maybe rather beautiful, I said.

I want to blame her but, as the unstable source of all chaos, she keeps slipping away. The other girls, she confided on another occasion – I don't think they like me. They have this false way of laughing. She imitated the laugh. A weak, spooky snigger. They're probably jealous, I said. Natalie Green's lipo hasn't turned out as she hoped, Jude said. She sobs in the girls' toilets about her elastic stocking. Jude's disclosures came, vivid and separate. In an instant she could put on a teacher. It was like watching a clip from a film. The performance was brief, effective and over.

I see my young self in Jude though I can't connect her relationship with my son to my first boyfriend – Ben Allardyce with the hairless legs and strawberry-blond ringlets. No doubt there is a protective taboo mechanism at work that keeps memory and the next generation from cross-contamination. Youth in a parent-proof bottle. I am dressed up in my old school uniform and chewing gum, only the clothes do not quite fit and the face on top of the pale blue shirt and wonky tie is no longer fresh and has a misleading air of sophistication that I never possessed. I come from an earlier, freer generation; some kind of hey-nonny-no time when young people were unbridled and their university fees paid for. There are photos from this era that are indeed risible. Four inches square and bathed in a Lucozade glow of sunset light caused by the fading of the print colour. The pair of us, Ben Allardyce and I, hand in hand, peer out through hair and smoke, looking either sullen or manic and dressed in outrageous garments. We met in Tottenham Court Road – an app-free, Internet-free pick-up. Ben was on his way from HMV in Oxford Street, I from Middlesex Hospital where I had been visiting a friend who was recovering from peritonitis. Both establishments – the hospital and the biggest music shop in Britain – are now closed; the hospital razed to the ground and replaced by luxury apartments. I saw Ben before he saw me. He was silently arguing with himself or some invisible person as he walked along. His hands chopped the air in school debating society gestures. I smiled. Dressed in a black leather fedora with brass studs round the hatband, a man's striped jacket and an ultra-short, tiered denim skirt, I was highly visible. Nothing less than a bed sheet descending and draping itself over my head would have concealed me. After a short and enigmatic conversation of the do-I-know-you type, he marched me along in the direction I was going; punishment, I think, for catching him out and smirking. We went to the nearest pub for a drink. It was an unattractive barn of a place with a clientele of silent alcoholics and tourists who had strayed from theatre land. We sat in a corner under a pair of tarnished brass sconces topped by red-fringed shades. Dingy wallpaper, on the tobacco-brown spectrum, deepened in colour nearer the ceiling. I was beguiled by my boldness in allowing the encounter while knowing that the boy and I shared the tame protection of parents, school and broad daylight. A different set of rules has to be broken to meet a stranger, I thought. After a few sips of beer and a drag on Ben's cigarette, I dropped the supercilious smile.

I lean over and feel for the glass of water that is by the bed. I take a few gulps, put the glass back and curl on my side. I close my right nostril with my ring finger and breathe through the left. A practice that is supposed to stop the mind forming words.

47

They arrive just before twelve-thirty on Sunday, William and Jane. He is wearing his brown corduroy suit, and she, having taken off a light but warm Puffa coat, reveals calf-length culottes and a fur-trimmed cardigan to which is pinned an astonishingly large, flat brooch in a dull metal that at first glance I take to be something medical.

William is full of good cheer and Jane Brims quietly polite and pleased to be here. So much so, that, as I take her coat from her and let it hang almost weightless over my arm, I jump to the conclusion that they are here to announce their engagement. I put my money on William taking the lead and Jane Brims coyly shimmering with happiness. A quick check of the woman's hands, as she expresses her appreciation of the smells coming from the kitchen, shows a piece of rose quartz set in silver and a spirally ring like a snake, both of which she was wearing when we first met. This proves nothing though since, while the news is fresh, a ring might remain in the shop being made larger or smaller, or, given Jane Brims's taste for contemporary jewellery, designed from scratch as a special commission. As the parties concerned are of a certain age, both ring and engagement might be dispensed with but I suspect that Jane Brims will milk the occasion for all it is worth. The question is when the announcement will be made.

I settle my father and Jane Brims in the living room, pour them each a large glass of wine and place a bowl of olives in front of them. From the kitchen I hear the pair of them talking. Jane's fluty voice dominates my father's lower notes. I move around, uncoordinated, in an atmosphere hazy with steam. I crush pistachio nuts with a rolling pin and forget the oil that heats to smoking point while my back is turned. I have a coughing fit. I slam the frying pan into the sink and turn on the tap. The fat hisses and spurts as the pan overflows with copious cold water.

At one-thirty, the food is ready to dish up. I go into the living room and immediately notice Jane's socks. They are the same, or similar, floral-patterned socks, that she wore when I first encountered her. This time, I see them in their entirety, heels, toes, the lot, because Jane Brims has discarded her shoes. These are not in evidence and I wonder whether she left them neatly by the front door though I have no recall of that, nor is our house the type to inspire meticulousness. I was so preoccupied with looking at Jane's fingers that I missed what was going on at floor level. I take the shoelessness as a bad sign. My father has his stout brown lace-ups on and the contrast between him sitting squarely on the sofa, properly shod, and Jane Brims at ease next to him in the culottes, one foot tucked under her, the other seductively nudged up against one of William's ankles, evokes, grotesquely, Manet's painting, *Le Déjeuner sur l'herbe*. I have the role of the unseen person who causes the naked woman and the clothed man on the left to turn and look out of the picture with expressions of charming receptiveness. I hasten down the garden to the wooded grove out of sight of the house to announce that the meal is ready. Like rabbits, Liz said. Surely not . . . they are in the front room . . . Jane is wearing culottes.

William and Jane rise and cross the living room in a series of fussy movements. I cover the dining table with a cloth and leave a heap of cutlery at the far end for hasty distribution in case anyone should join us. The last thing I want is to sit staring at empty place settings. I seat William at the head of the table with Jane round the corner next to him. That way, if no one else turns up we can be cosy together at one end. I use the word though I feel as cosy as a cat in a bucket of water. I remain standing.

'Well, you'll never guess where we went on Friday, or whom we saw.' William chuckles as he settles himself.

'Peterborough. We went to Peterborough. Jane wanted to look round the cathedral. In particular, she wanted to see the rood. Who was the sculptor of the Christ figure, Jane?'

'Frank Roper. Roper as in rope,' Jane says.

'It's done in gilded aluminium. Immense. Very glittery, very modern. Jane liked it. We saw Hugh. What do you think of that?'

'Astonishing. How was he?'

'He was on good form. I rang him up. On Thursday evening, after I'd spoken to you. And I got him! That was quite something, wasn't it?'

'It was,' I say.

'We caught the three minutes past ten from King's Cross and were in Peterborough forty-seven minutes later. It was one of these new-fangled trains with the seats all facing the same way, like an aeroplane. And fast. It belted along. We arrived in time for a cup of coffee and a leisurely look round the cathedral. Hugh drove into town and met us for one o'clock lunch at a Chinese place in the Broadway. He gave good instructions and we found it with no trouble. A former Nat West bank. You could still make out the lettering on the façade.'

I last saw my brother at Helena's funeral. He had shaved his head. He wore a diagonally striped tie and smelled faintly of lemongrass.

'What was his news?' I ask.

'He's been in Kuala Lumpur. Combined it with a holiday in Penang. Jet-skiing and parasailing. Apparently you wear some harness contraption and get pulled a thousand feet in the air by a hydraulic winch. I must say it wouldn't suit me.'

'Who did he go with?'

'As far as I know, he was on his own. He enjoys these sporting activities.'

Jane sips her wine. She holds back – graciously – her gaze fixed on a point somewhere in the middle of the room below the central light fitting; the spot where house flies circle on a hot summer's day. Let him say his piece, her expression says. I can be patient.

I have to admit that William is his normal self. Although he participates in uncharacteristic behaviour – going to *Sweeney Todd* and regimental exhibitions – his speech and manner are the same. Jane has introduced new pastimes but nothing else is different and so far she has not modified his wardrobe. If she's made him a present of a Nehru jacket or a Fair Isle tank top, he does not wear it.

Had my mother been with us, the conversation would at this moment have branched out into speculation about Hugh's personal life; the mystery of it. Who or what he is concealing. In her discourse with my brother, her sharp ears listened out for a first-person plural but Hugh never slipped up, or only when speaking of himself and others in a collective predicament; stuck in a traffic jam or held up on the tarmac. Did he go to the cinema on his own, go-karting, paragliding – *every* time? Even tennis appeared to be solo. It wasn't possible to play tennis alone – unless against a wall – my mother said. Surely even Hugh didn't play tennis with a wall.

William hung back on the subject of his son. He neither disapproved nor joined in when my mother probed the situation. In the face of his tolerance, I am unable to pursue further details of the life and happiness of my brother.

William starts to tell of the town museum in Peterborough.

Jane Brims interrupts. 'I was disappointed not to see the mural decoration at Longthorpe Tower. The Wheel of Life and the Wheel of the Five Senses. In particular, I should like to have seen the frieze of birds.' Her mouth forms words with little munching motions.

'Longthorpe Tower is shut during the week. Open at weekends and on bank holidays. It couldn't be helped,' William chips in.

'Paintings of local birds from the Fenland. Bittern, curlew, swans and various kinds of geese.'

'Excuse me for interrupting, Jane. I need to tell the others that lunch is ready – and rescue the food.'

I go halfway up the staircase and call out. A smell of burnt oil hangs in the air. No one replies. I loathe everyone currently in the house. My sons, my father, Jude, Jane Brims. I should have said no to William. I do not want an extra person here. It is not a question of cooking: I cannot sustain the semi-formality imposed by this woman. I cannot be the hybrid beast of polite hostess with a friendly wagging tail. Not this weekend.

I consider escape – out and away down Dairyman's Road – but go on up to the bathroom and examine my grim face in the mirror. In youth any old expression will do but by the time you get to my age the mind in the eyes and the set of the jaw are more significant than any beauty regime and these, together with an air of tranquillity, are what mark out the girls from the soon-to-be fruitcakes. As I pencil lines around my eyes and rub this and that into my flesh, I become a little more colourful but fail the test. I look older than Jane Brims.

A phone is lying on the shelf above the basin. Jude's. I pick it up. There are times when the hand is out of step with the brain.

48

The chair, of the standard polypropylene type ubiquitous in schools, featured in Jude's first photograph. I sat on one in the IT suite the other afternoon. Single mould on a welded frame with a window at the sitter's lower-back position. A window, not for looking through, but to provide a hand-hold for easier carrying and stacking. There would be other ways of carrying the chair; by the seat and held in front like a tea tray, by the top and dragged behind along the floor. I had not known which it was. Jude showed the latest picture to Randal. I did not want to see it. I do not want to see it now. Alan Child drags the chair.

Every day this scene is acted out. The detail varies and the setting. A hotel room. A cliff. A bridge. Preceded by other actions. Sometimes an entry in a newspaper states what happened. Usually not, unless the person is famous. I should have told Jude to delete the chair; to delete all the pictures on her phone of the former stationery cupboard and Alan Child going into it. I am sick at what my son has done.

My finger slithers over the screen and suddenly I see Jude in her home clothes – scarf, jumper, jeans, socks – sitting cross-legged on the floor with her back against a bed, Ewan beside her. The background is evening dark. I feel as light as a shuttlecock, wildly hit, that flies out of a game. It is as if I have seen a pair of ghosts. The faces, lit by a white-tinged glare, are pale. The eyes stare out. The scarf wound round and round Jude's neck is like a protective cowl. I let the glow of the screen die in my hand. The phone goes back on the shelf.

If I had not touched the phone this would not have happened, I think, as I creep downstairs to the kitchen. I dish up and unsteadily carry plates of salmon, potato and broccoli through to the living room.

I announce that we should begin without the children. 'Bon appétit,' I say. 'It's lovely you're here. Do begin.'

'Begin a meal, start a car. Quite right,' my father says.

He reaches inside his jacket pocket for his reading glasses, raises them to his face and puts them on aslant with the earpieces not around his ears but jammed higher up his head. I look at them in bewilderment. They are chunky, green framed, and turn my father into a panto-mime dame.

'They're Mum's, aren't they?' I say.

'Mislaid mine. These do,' he says.

'I like your plum-coloured walls,' Jane said. 'I like

strong colour in a dining room.' She treats me to a brisk smile and picks up her knife and fork. She separates particles of nut from the fish and moves them to the side of her plate. They form a little heap.

We talk but I take nothing in. We have reached the pudding stage when I hear Ross's bedroom door close and footsteps on the stairs.

'That's Ross and Jude,' I say. 'Jude will be leaving. She never stops for Sunday lunch.'

'They'll say hello,' my father says. 'Then Ross will join us.'

It is not a question. Though much has changed since he was young, William considers it unthinkable that a child of a family, or the child's guest, will walk straight through a hall and out of the door, without looking in. I see both points of view but come down on the side of old manners.

'Come and say hello,' I call – without conviction.

I hear a hushed scuffle and then silence.

'Ross?'

He appears. He nods through the greetings.

'Jude's going,' he says.

'Is she there?' Jane asks. 'We'd like to see her.' She puts on her smile.

Ross takes a step back. 'Jude?' he says.

We wait. Through the gap of the door jamb, I see the shadow of Jude's coat.

The delay is long but then Ross re-enters and Jude is next to him.

'You're not stopping to eat with us, Jude? The crumble is really delicious,' Jane says.

She questions the young people about their studies and intentions, oblivious to the blank panic on their faces. If she is aware, she proceeds cruelly. The single-word replies that Ross gives do not lead to conversation. Jude is silent. At one point, Ross reaches for her hand but she does not take it.

'Do you have brothers or sisters, Jude?' Jane asks.

'A half-sister,' Jude whispers.

William leans forward and cups a hand around his ear.

'She lives in Barcelona?' I say.

'No. No, she doesn't. She lives in Vancouver. Her boyfriend's Canadian. She's older than me. My father was married before.' Jude speaks quickly. 'Now history's repeating itself.'

'Really?' Jane Brims leans forward eagerly. 'Well!' she says when it becomes clear that there is to be no further information.

'There's food in the kitchen. The fish might be a bit cold but it can soon be heated up. Veg. Pudding. Help yourselves,' I say.

'I have to go,' Jude says.

Ross follows her.

'Mm. *She's* a bit of a handful,' Jane says before the front door slams shut.

William looks baffled.

'I don't know what's going on,' I say.

Some kind of altercation is taking place outside. Jude is shouting that Ross should leave her alone. I look through the back window, as though that will deflect attention from what is plainly audible at the front. I survey the bikes haphazardly parked against the fence and their spokes full of leaves. I give the garden my full attention. Jane and my father start talking again. I join in and by then, whatever is happening in the street has stopped or moved on.

We finish the meal and get through coffee without an announcement of impending marriage. I remain keyed up; hardly able to concentrate. I have already dropped and broken the cream jug, cut myself with a paring knife and burnt my wrist taking a dish from the oven at the wrong angle. Luckily all three incidents took place out of sight in the kitchen but the pain from the burn continues.

49

At least they had their clothes on. The words once lodged in my head return like an irritating refrain, ba-dah, ba-dah, ba-dah-ba, bereft of meaning or consolation. Dissociated from any world I recognise, Jude and Ewan rested against a bed; Jude's expression neither happy, sad, forced, surprised nor intent – frankly inscrutable. She was the one with the arm out holding the phone. He smiled at the lens. Smiled. They sat pressed up against each other, every part of their sides touching, a situation that can happen in a posed photo. Move in, move in, the photographer says and I am hip to hip with the girl in my class I most dislike, or a besuited stranger who sports a pale carnation and smells of beer. I go back and forth, trying to work out when, how, how often, Ross? – and the hours pass. Is it possible that this was an isolated event? Is anything, ever? They chose to be close together. The bed had a white cover. It was not Ewan's bed. Something multicoloured intruded on a corner of the frame. It could have been a cushion or a discarded towel. Whatever it was, I did not recognise it.

The image of Ewan and Jude, like the image of the chair, fills a cinema screen in my mind. The next moment it becomes as tiny and potent as a letter on the bottom line of an optician's chart. I have no control over its size or focus.

Jude was shocked to overhear me talking to my son, my voice warm but somehow disembodied; the intonation of a mother talking to a baby and with the same lack of expectation of receiving a reply. Cleaning her teeth in the bathroom, she did not catch all the words. I seemed, at one point, to be saying something about a sick cat. She thought Ewan was dead and his room a shrine. Did she go and look, unglueing those parts of her body that adhered to Ross and easing herself out of bed? She would have hesitated at the foot of the space-saver stairs. Ewan's life was invisible to me. Up in the loft room. Out in the street. But invisibility is different from nothing. I assumed that his life consisted of nothing. I want normality for my sons; a mix, in proportions of conformity and non-conformity that most people arrive at. I am glad, in a way, that in his self-imposed exile at the top of the house Ewan has stayed in the flow. The toehold also seems to diminish him.

I flick through mental pictures. Ewan. Ewan and Jude. Ross. Ross and Jude. Ewan. In a train. On a park bench. Under a tree. Fast as animation. Enough. Two brothers. One girl.

I have kept all the children's books, those belonging to the boys and a few that have survived from my childhood. The story of Lieutenant Kijé is not among them. The book was borrowed and re-borrowed from the public library which is currently closed for the next fourteen months, possibly indefinitely, while the building it is part of – Southgate Town Hall – is redeveloped to accommodate private residential apartments. We used to go once a week. The boys pulled books out of the boxes, turned pages right to left, or left to right, and looked at the pictures. If we were not in a rush, I read whole stories to them. We sat on low benches. Ross on my knee, the other two, either side, pressed against me. Ross was obsessed by Lieutenant Kijé. I had a lot of explaining to do. Tsars, hussars, troikas, banishment, Siberia, pardons, promotions, heroes' funerals. My little boy took it all in. He knew about soldiers and writing words that come out wrong and making mistakes and dancing. He accepted falling in love and weddings and dying. But what tormented him was the trick of portraying a story that is a lie, inside a story. Lieutenant Kijé was there, plainly there, in the illustrations, but he did not exist. The pictures showed the life of a clerical error. Ross was outraged by Kijé with his pink cheeks, brown waif-like eyes and black curly hair. His bride decked out like a Russian doll. A snowy wasteland. The barred prison window. A gnawed crust of bread. He wanted pictures to depict what really happened. Might not that be dull, I suggested, page after page of Tsar Paul and his trusted group of soldiers in conversation about Kijé, the lieutenant who never existed and whose life they invented. Ross admitted it would be a bit boring, but better dull than *those* pictures. Had he known the words 'trumped up', he would have used them.

I stand at the top of the stairs intending to speak definitively of Jude. I knock on Ewan's door, step inside and open my mouth.

He is lying on the bed on top of the duvet. He props himself up on his elbows as if ready to listen to me. There is a naturalness to the posture. In a small room, unless you are Houdini, there are not so many options. You can sit at the desk, or on the floor with your back against a bed, or you can lie on the bed. I tell him about Jane Brims's visit. He laughs and when he speaks his voice is different. He is more alert. Sheepish? Do I imagine that? Like Dirk Neerhoff, I am looking for clarity.

50

If Sunday evening were a location it would be a harbour wall by an estuary, tidal water slapping against stone. The ferry timetable on a board attached to a post: '10–11 and 3–4 daily. Monday to Saturday. Wave or phone for service.' The far shore is visible, similar to where I stand but out of reach. It is a nothing kind of time, a little moribund, and usually I watch television. I cannot do this simple, mindless thing and instead go from the kitchen to the living room and back, on patrol. I clear the table and the coffee cups and wash the pans in three-minute bursts, then I am off again. Occasionally, I stop mid-step, as though a gate bars the way.

As I bump against the stack of boxes and set the clock chiming, I see my mother standing – she rarely sat down – standing in a room, gesticulating; her face animated and her hair that was rather wild and unruly springing from her head and contributing to her vitality. She reminded me of one of William Blake's angel figures who fizz and spark – so different from the Victorian hymnbook types who seem to be waiting beyond endurance in a queue.

I fetch a heavy-duty screwdriver from the tool kit under the kitchen table, slide the blade under the staples that fasten the lid of the uppermost box and prise until the released ends stick up, sharp and dangerous. I pull the cardboard sections apart, with a noise of tearing. There are the pair of Afghan rug cushions that used to be on a window seat in my parents' old house. The colours are good: faded indigo, terracotta and saffron yellow. I take out the cushions and hug them to myself. They have a musty smell of trapped dust. I have lost the modulations of Mum's voice though phrases and favourite words come through. It was not anything she said that comforted me, but rather her presence.

I go into the living room, carrying the cushions in my arms. I place them at one end of the sofa, lie down and rest my head on the prickly fabric. I do not know how long I stay there, stretched out as much as the sofa's length will allow, but at a certain point I hear people talking a few feet away. The insistent timbre of their voices is wrong for a dream. I realise that I am hearing recorded sound and that the television must be on. I swivel round and swing my feet onto the floor. I quickly become immersed, not so much in what is going on, but in the emotional tone of the film. I am drawn into the made-up world as to a view of the sea that distracts and appeases and on which I can gaze for a while. I missed the beginning but that does not seem to matter. While I was lying prostrate and mentally absent, something happened, a murder or a kiss, that is not reprised, or even alluded to, but which creates an atmosphere. The film is bathed in an atmosphere that is, in effect, an aftermath.

When I finally drag myself to bed I am unable to sleep. I remember only the bad parts of my life. At four in the morning, I go downstairs. I put on a jumper that I have left hanging over a kitchen chair and slip on a pair of old espadrilles that I keep by the back door. I draw the bolts and go out into the garden. I find the broom and begin to sweep. Fallen leaves and sycamore helicopters. A pink plastic clothes peg. Something glints. A knife that must have been dropped on a rare summer day when we ate outside. I pick it up, put it by the back step and carry on sweeping. Having cleared the accessible section in the middle of the garden, I tackle the edges. I lift the bikes away from the fence and shift the barbecue. The pile of fallen leaves grows. I breathe the cool air, glad to be out of doors.

By first light, the paving slabs, after my obsessive tidying, resemble a beach swept clean by the tide. Creeping plants, trails of green set free from accumulated debris, push up through the cracks. I start to pull up last summer's geraniums from the tubs. One or two are in flower though the scarlet of the blooms, over-wintered, has lost intensity and acquired a purplish tinge. I cut the stems and put them to one side to stick in a jug indoors. The rest go into a black plastic rubbish bag. I never got myself to Crews Hill or any other nursery to buy spring bulbs.

I keep glancing up at the house.

51

At seven o'clock on Monday morning, I go in to Ross. I have had so little sleep. I move as though I have been knocked down by a slow-moving vehicle that failed to kill or injure me but left me nervously impaired. I stand over the concealed corpse in the bed and address it. There is still time, I tell the corpse. Time to compose an apology. It can be brief; handwritten or electronic. If handwritten, it can be taken along to Mr Goode's secretary. Mr Goode need not be encountered. If electronic, fine. In both cases, getting up must take place, school clothes be put on, a journey to Lloyd-Barron Academy undertaken in the old way. The five days are up. I continue to talk as I open the curtains, find underpants, socks, shirt, tie, trousers, blazer and place them on a chair. I speak of bravery, adulthood, self-interest – and finally of necessity. I lean over to pull off the duvet but some movement in the air or perhaps my smell, the smell of mother, as I draw close causes a Moro reflex in the body, a tight monkey grip. The bedding, previously loose, convulses. It billows and hardens under my hand. I cannot wrestle this cumbersome thing into school uniform or drag it along the street. If it doesn't budge, it doesn't budge.

I shut the front door and set off into the ordinary morning. Dairyman's Road, Alderman's Hill, Palmers Green station. The air is a salve and the gardens I pass, for the first time this year, have the cool, sweet smell of spring vegetation. Every step takes me further away from home. I am glad that this is so, though I carry its inhabitants with me and am bound to return. I understand traumatic bonding, though someone more of a Puritan might call it perseverance; words and actions interminably repeated. A child does, in the end, lose interest in the power sockets. I undertake my visits, or visitations, to Ewan's room and Ross's room in that spirit. Here we go again. It causes less anguish than thinking afresh. I keep walking. I think of the academy – another school day – and wonder what is happening there. I should like to talk to Ginny but the tone of my last conversation with her prevents me. I am afraid of her disapproval, though I share it. I keep walking.

I have to prepare for a budget meeting on Tuesday and this occupies me. I do not get round to more mundane tasks until late in the afternoon. Among my emails, there is a message from Tony Goode.

Good morning,

*After due consideration, the five days being actioned,
whilst an exclusion may be an appropriate sanction,
warranting the severity of the misdemeanour and
bearing in mind that malicious communication is
setting a precedent, the Academy takes into
consideration any contributing factors that are identified after an incident of behaviour has occurred. For
example, where a student has suffered bereavement,
has mental health issues or has been subject to
bullying. In the lenient circumstances of the object of
the malicious communication being unfortunately
deceased and presumably harassment, cause offence,
inconvenience or needless anxiety not being applicable
in the circumstances, could yourself and Ross Doig
report to my office on Monday morning at 08.30*

I read the message through twice. I think it means
what I take it to mean. I am puzzled that it has only just
reached me. It is dated today. I can only assume that the
text was drafted on Friday but withheld until approved
by somebody – and then forgotten about.

I call Lloyd-Barron Academy.

'Thank you for waiting. What's the name again?
Barrie?'

'No, Parry.'

'Parry?'

'Yes. But it's about Ross Doig. DOIG. I have received the email about my son Ross Doig's reinstatement and we're so delighted and relieved that he can—'

'They've put you through to the wrong extension. Try the other number. There's no way back on this one. No worries.' Me, I'll carry on chatting or eating a banana.

I call again. The phone rings twice, followed by an out-of-office reply. Back to the switchboard. I finally get Amrita.

'Mr Goode is in a meeting,' she says in a hushed voice.

I say that perhaps she, Amrita, can help me. I have received the email about my son Ross Doig's reinstatement.

'Please hold the line,' she says.

I hear scratching, rustling sounds like hens moving about in a coop, then a long silence.

'Hello.'

'Hello.'

I am on the point of giving up when Amrita comes back.

I begin again, determined to keep going this time even if I am communing with chickens. I say that I am delighted and relieved that Ross can continue his studies in the school that has done so much for him and where he's been so happy. He and his brothers. It has been a long association. He really has learned his lesson and the

248

academy won't regret the decision. I am only sorry that we didn't get the message in time for Ross and me to keep the appointment at eight-thirty. Obviously, I've been checking my emails on an hourly basis but for some inexplicable reason it has only just shown up. We'll be there first thing tomorrow and I'm really sorry for any mix-up.

I hear the scratching sound, followed by a whisper. Someone coughs.

'Oh, have you only just got the email? I'll let Mr Goode know. I'm looking at Tuesday's agenda . . . bear with me . . . No, Mr Goode has an appointment tomorrow morning. Tell Ross to be here for registration as usual. I'll revert to you if Mr Goode wishes to arrange a meeting.'

I thank Amrita – excessively.

52

I feel hopeful as I travel home. When I enter the house I call out hello. I am a mother with children at home. Two of them. A double bill for my performance as actor nurse. Nurse Actor. The hall smells rancid, of fishy broccoli like an unappetising hospital lunch.

I go upstairs. Ross's door is shut. I stare at the old torn-off stickers, the shards of colour like fragments of butterfly wings, and try to recall what was once depicted. I practise a few of Professor Martinez's expressions. Confidently unexpectant. Unexpectantly confident. Bland as hell. I open the door.

'Did you get my text?'

Ross is sitting on the floor, squashed in a space between his bed and the chest of drawers. His shoulders are draped in a green fringed silk shawl that belonged to my grandmother. In his hands is a carved wooden tortoise and on the floor next to him two more tortoises in diminishing sizes. He has been rummaging through the boxes. He is a child.

'Good news, isn't it?' I say.

The sound he makes is not the full nuh-hah; it is closer to no.

It's all right, Ross. You can go back. I stuck to what was simple and important. I did not suggest that he can put the grim episode behind him, or that he has got off lightly. I made no reference to normality. We/you can get back to normal. I never use the expression as I know that boys fear what mothers consider normal. I was careful with the words because the smallest mistake can turn text into a pretext.

He did not reply and he is not replying now but that is not significant. I am amazed that Mr Goode has not insisted on the written apology. He must have forgotten he demanded one. Ross is bloody lucky.

I am on the point of leaving when he opens his mouth.

'It isn't all right.'

'Sorry, darling?'

'You said, "It's all right."'

'Yes? Are you making an objection?'

'It's a lie. It isn't all right and never will be.'

I tell him not to be absurd. I say I'm sorry that I put a foot wrong. He's been punished and it's over. I tell him not to get entrenched in a foolish position and that I'm not even listening any longer. He is wrapped in green silk and sitting cross-legged. His expression is not that

251

of the Buddha. I say that he will see things differently by the morning. I am tired.

Tuesday is the day of the budget meeting. I immerse myself in work. I have no idea whether Ross will see sense during the course of the day. I do not communicate with him. I stay in the office until seven o'clock and am glad when the Victoria line train waits at Euston so that the service can be regulated and again in the tunnel outside Highbury and Islington for a platform to become available. I stop off at the supermarket to buy extra food because Ross cleared the fridge yesterday. I choose the longest queue at the checkout. My capacity to distance myself has the staying power of a dandelion clock. As soon as I step into Ross's room, I see from the taut muscles in his neck, the rigid set of his head on his shoulders, that he has not relented. I wear myself out with cajoling and threatening. I speak of prosecution and parenting orders. I tell him I will not cover up for him. On the contrary, I will inform the school of his stupidity. This is motherhood as extreme sport. It is one of the vilest evenings of my life.

On Wednesday, as usual, I have a stack of emails. There is one from Chris Orrick. I haven't seen or heard from him for months but it is clear from the message that he believes he is in the forefront of my mind.

Hi Lorna, you must be wondering why you haven't been sent a copy of my book. Joking. No, actually, I'm thinking the Stratford Tube Crash of 8th April 1953 has better potential. I've figured out how it's going to work. A damaged signal on permanent red, the train driver's vision obscured by a cloud of dust. A similar accident happened at that precise location seven years previously. Perfect ingredients. I'm the driver, right. Suddenly everything feels weird, different. In front of the cab is a jagged hole, belching out smoke. An eerie light I've never seen before . . .

I leave a message on the academy's answerphone, saying that Ross has flu. This is despicable but buys us a little time. He has imposed an additional ordeal on himself, some made-up, painful thing that he has to go through and that I have to go through because we are connected and I am responsible for him.

I visit the page of the Lloyd-Barron Academy website that deals with attendance and absenteeism. Zero tolerance, written in bold, jumps from the screen. I laugh. I could have predicted the term, embraced by New York cops and petty office tyrants the world over, though my cynicism has a masochistic kick to it that strengthens when, delving further, I find that support and help for vulnerable students can be obtained from the LBA Family Advocate, Mary de Silva, by appointment. I laugh like a madwoman.

I check my diary. A virulent strain of flu, followed by post-viral fatigue, should take us to the Easter holidays. I also see that Oliver's term is about to end. I had forgotten about Oliver. I send him a text saying that I can pick him up next Saturday, or Sunday. Name a time. The prospect of setting off alone along the A23 is blissful.

The rest of the week goes by more temperately. I am amazed as I have been in the past that adjustments to new, undesirable circumstances can be made. My appetite is reduced and my sleep pattern poor but I go to work, prepare food, stick laundry in the washing machine and dishes in the dishwasher, shove a damp cloth over the kitchen surfaces. I communicate with my sons. I do not hate them. I touch their hair and share a joke. I raise blinds and open curtains. I pick up used mugs from the floor.

Ross tries to take a plate of beef stew out of the kitchen. I forbid it. On this I am firm. I cannot allow him to eat his dinner in his bedroom. We wrestle over the full plate, tugging in opposite directions as the contents slop and slide. Ross shouts obscenities and I yell, 'Did you feel good when you wrote that bile?' Globs of meat and carrot land on the floor. My phone beeps. It is a text from Oliver. He will go straight from Brighton to Cornwall. Night diving again. The details that I looked up in September return to me. The dead men's fingers, the chimney cave, the cauldron with vertical sides, the former MoD range station where the divers set out from. I recall the word 'gully'. I think of entanglements with nets and lines, torch failure, the perils of getting lost in the dark. Seawater is bone cold in spring. I begin to cry. Ross leaves the room. I hold onto the edge of the table while I heave and sob. Then stop. I cannot bring my middle son home. I wipe my face, pick up the phone and call Randal. As soon as I hear his evening-at-home voice, I realise I could have managed alone. I sense that I have made a bad situation worse but, having spoken, I can't go back. He will set off directly after lunch tomorrow. For the first time since he left I have asked for his help.

53

'Ewan's out. Ross is here, though.'

'He's the one I've come to see.' Randal's expression is purposeful as he places his helmet on the floor and removes his motorcycling jacket. 'Better have a word with you first before I go up. I need the full picture.'

'OK.'

Randal has had a new, boyish haircut. Classy. I am wearing crystal dangly earrings and a top that I discarded and then rescued from the bag destined for the charity shop. The top is black with a silver thread running through it. Randal's surprised glance when he straightens up confirms that I look like a half-decorated Christmas tree.

'Jude?' he says.

He climbs out of the biker's trousers, more adeptly this time though I detect a certain geriatric stiffness in his right knee.

'Not here.'

'Any particular reason? I thought she stayed over at the weekend.'

'She didn't turn up.'

'Right.' He shepherds me into the living room and closes the door behind him. 'Sit down, Lorna. We need to do this properly.'

He indicates the dining table and we sit down opposite each other. He has arrived from North Hertfordshire and is sorting out our problems.

I have already given a brief outline of events on the phone but I go over them again. He lets me speak without interrupting and his expression becomes increasingly stern.

'*When* exactly did they exclude him?'

I give him the date.

'You should have involved me right away.'

'Would it have made any difference?'

'Well, yes. It might have done. But we don't know now, do we? We're another stage on.'

'We are.'

'Does he say why he won't go back to school?'

'No.'

'Have you any idea why not?'

'Pride, humiliation, shame – those kinds of things.'

'He'll have to get over them, won't he? I'll go and speak to him.' Randal stands up. 'Is there anything else I should know?'

'I don't think so. Oh, he asked me not to tell you.'

'I bet he did. And does he now know I know?'

I shake my head.

'Good. Did you know there's a scratch there?' He points at a particular spot on the table.

'There are probably several. I haven't counted recently.'

'Pity. It was a good table.'

He goes upstairs. I hear the knock and then the door shuts. I get up, close the living-room door and turn on the television. I do not want to hear the muffled sound of Randal's voice, or Ross's indecipherable replies, or failures to reply – or shouting. Raised male voices that explode and reverberate like a cathedral organ in a space suited to a harmonium. A woman in Edwardian-style drag is playing a tack piano. Her hands shimmy up and down the keyboard. The tinny music is insistent enough to overcome normal levels of talk from upstairs though not an uproar. Then she starts to sing. I thought as I bedecked myself in the crystal earrings that the day might end up in Accident and Emergency at North Middlesex University Hospital. A huge motorbike in the front garden, chained to the gatepost. A defiant son in the back bedroom.

'Oh, the TV's on. Is this a documentary?'

'Probably,' I say. 'It doesn't look like drama.'

Randal comes over and sits down next to me on the sofa. The leather squeaks and I feel a slight rebound on my side. For a couple of minutes we both stare at the screen. The entertainer bashes out the chorus of 'My Old Man Said Follow the Van'. Her audience is a small and unresponsive audience of old folk. One ancient lady begins to tap the arm of her wheelchair.

'Actually, I think I might have seen this before.' I click the remote and kill the scene dead. 'So, how did you get on?'

'He says he's got a headache. I didn't get much out of him.'

'You said your bit and he said nothing?'

'That's about it. But, hey, I might have done some good. I'll go up again and have another go. See if anything I said has sunk in.'

I nod.

'What about you? Are you still sleeping badly?' He takes a good look at me.

'Oh, it got better, then it came back. It's not bad sleep. I just wake at half-past four. I get up. It's dark.'

'Of course it is. Stop in bed. You'll never break the pattern if you keep getting up. Don't open your eyes. What do you do, anyway, at that time in the morning?'

'I come downstairs and read. Sit in front of the oven. I'm getting through a lot of books.'

'I don't care how many books you're getting through. You'll turn into a ghost.'

We sit in silence, thinking our own thoughts, I suppose, but each also conscious that the other is there.

'Sad words when they'll never go home again, drunk or sober,' I say. 'The song,' I add, since Randal looks baffled.

'Oh, that. Yes. Why do people always assume that when you get to a hundred you'll develop a liking for old-time music hall? It's more likely that our current centenarians listened to Tommy Steele and Danny Kaye, isn't it?'

'"Little White Bull"?' As I say the words, I feel an urge to put a hand on Randal's thigh. The impulse – it can no longer be called a habit – disconcerts me. Is it triggered by some verbal prompt, in which case, what? Bull? I stand up and go and sit in the armchair.

'What's the matter?'

'Nothing.'

'You're jumpy.' Randal leans back and locks his hands behind his head. 'I could get into that stuff. I'll spend my final years in *Downton Abbey* or *The Forsyte Saga*. I must buy a collared waistcoat.' He unclasps his hands. 'So is Jude coming round later?'

'I honestly don't know. You've already asked that.' I pause. 'Did your brother fancy me?'

'Michael? What? Where's that come from?'

'Just answer.'

'Well, I'd say absolutely not.'

'Oh. OK. You're probably right.'

'Have you heard from him or something?'

I consider this and think back to the last time I heard from Mike Doig. I seem to remember that I sent a birthday card the year after Randal left. Mike used to pull up outside the house in a volley of hooting. He once ate twelve barbecued pork sausages. I do not think I ever had a serious conversation with him. It was nothing but jokes with Mike.

'Lorna?'

'No, of course not. I don't mean now. I meant years ago. When we were young.'

'Same. Same answer. You were never his type, Lorna.'

'I wasn't? What was his type?' I feel faintly miffed.

'Well, Marilyn, I suppose. Or Susie. What's this about?'

'Nothing. I was thinking of brothers and relationships and rivalry. In general, you know. I live with these boys but I don't really grasp what goes on between them.'

'Of course you do. This is just navel-gazing. You go in for these intellectual sideshows.' Randal picks up his phone. His thumb slides and his face relaxes as he communes with a different world. 'By the way, we're still young,' he says, without looking up.

He could never stand to be in the same room as his brother and mother. Individually, yes. Together, no. Ursula has dementia now so the situation might have eased. I consider asking after her but hold back. The conversation always ends up in the same place with Randal saying, 'I've told Charmian to shoot me.'

'Jude was here last weekend – but things were rocky,' I say.

'She's cute.' His hand still busy with the phone.

'Cute?'

'Yes, she is. She's more mature than Ross, that's perfectly—'

I cut in. 'Yes, it was clear to me—'

'Oh, calm down, Lorna.' He sets the phone down.

I take a few deep breaths.

A slow smile spreads across Randal's face.

'What's funny?'

'I get it. Why didn't you just tell me? That's great, isn't it? I'm really glad to hear he shows signs of life.'

I glance at the door to make sure that it is properly shut.

'I always guessed a girl was at the bottom of his troubles. He's come out of it. That's good. I thought he looked brighter. I said so, didn't I, last time I was here? You're ridiculous, Lorna. This is fantastic news. Ewan fancies the girl. So what? For once he's animated and you come down on him like a ton of bricks.'

I take a few breaths. 'They are brothers. They're meant to look out for each other.'

'They're young. These things happen. But *has* anything happened? Why are you being so bloody cagey? One minute it's supposition and the next you're hinting at wife stealing. In a way, he's quite glamorous, our eldest son. He's on the premises. It's natural that a girl would be curious about him. At the same age, you would have been the same. He's shagging her? I suppose that might be a bit awkward. On or off the premises?'

'I don't speculate,' I hiss through bared teeth.

'And Ross? What does he think's going on?'

'I've no idea.'

'It'll resolve itself.'

'These things always do?'

'Don't look at me like that. Yes, sooner or later they do. Situations of high tension find release. Where are you in all this? You've been locked in this weird bonding thing with Ewan. You're just pissed off he's cutting loose.'

'That's the front door. Here he is.' I get up. 'I'm going to find out where he's been.'

'Lorna,' Randal says in a warning voice.

Soft, regular steps, lighter than Ross's, cross the hall. Through the gap at the door jamb, I see someone pass. The kettle is switched on. Then the toaster. The fridge door thuds as it is shut. I smell burnt crumbs.

There is a kink in the ground-floor layout of the Dairyman's Road houses. The stairs stand in the way of a clear sightline from the front door to the kitchen. The passage lies offset to one side. I have no more than a tunnelled view when I step into the hall. I see one half of the back door, the end of the table that sticks out, and part of the dresser.

No one is visible – and then he is. He takes a mug and a plate from the dresser shelves. He is ordinary, lovable, nothing remarkable. He goes accompanied by a collection of sad shadows. His hair is at its longest. Ewan looks, whatever the weather, as if he has been left out in the rain.

54

The thing is, nothing beats family life. The three of us are sitting at the kitchen table on a Saturday afternoon. You do not need a fissure in the earth's crust opening up under the Central line. Accident, medical emergency, death, betrayal, or news of any of these, they can all happen at home. My discovery of Charmian – source of delight, according to the *Name Your Baby* book – involved a phone in the bathroom, as did my second foray into spying, though on neither occasion did I act with intent. Like a master key, shock unlocks some barrier in perception. Time collapses. Can't wait to see you Cx. There is always another world through the mirror, on the far side of the wardrobe, when the clock strikes thirteen. Over in that place, Frances Bennet is not with the horses.

Randal used to take Ewan out for a couple of hours on a Saturday afternoon to give me a break. He pushed the buggy to Grovelands Park and walked round the lake edged with willows and alders, or along Whappooles Bourne, the stream that flows down the steps of the dam and on through the wood, over gently sloping land.

Sometimes he went further afield, pounding along suburban streets. Many of these too in their names recall the old streams, Wellfield, Cranbourne, Muswell. The land was once criss-crossed with water. Silent water, moving or still, that reflected the sky; gurgling, bubbling water in wells and sluices; stagnant ponds. Their courses are now built over and trapped in pipes and culverts. Traffic rolls over them. The Muswell stream that sprang from a mossy well and was believed to have healing properties emerges at Palmers Green bus garage and empties into Pymmes Brook.

Later when Ewan could walk and talk there was more to do, frogs to find, sticks to pick up, but it is the early stage I recall, man and child setting off. In the rain, buggy hood up, plastic cover on, baby shielded and Randal in his waterproofs.

I have tried to imagine what it might feel like if Ewan lived with his father. Not that he has ever offered. The room at the top of the house empty. The problem parked elsewhere. Ewan wandering by the River Stort instead of around North London. The images have merged: Randal with the buggy and Ewan on muddy footpaths. I have never held my loved ones in mind statically, as though trapped in still photographs. They set off. They are free to go. I am not a GPS tracking device.

Ewan has a mouthful of toast. He chews and swallows

before replying to Randal's question about what he has done today. He mutters that he went for a run and then has to repeat it because Randal does not catch what he says.

'How many K?'

'Five or six.'

'Not bad. All on pavement?'

'No. It's a woodland trail. Part peat, part woodchip.'

'Nice,' Randal says approvingly. 'Where were you?'

Ewan chews again, wipes his mouth with the back of his hand. 'Some of it was a bit slippery.' He reaches for the butter. 'Northaw Great Wood.'

'Oh, out Cuffley way. You should try the Pacific Crest Trail. One of my colleagues does the PCT every year. Mexico to Canada. Two thousand, six hundred and fifty miles, in twenty-nine sections of doable lengths. I think he's done seven.'

'Cool.'

'Do you record your data, mileage and so on?'

'Not really.'

'No?'

'I can't see the point.'

'It's not a bad idea. You can set yourself new chal-lenges. I bought this for myself the other day.' Randal hitches up the cuff of his shirt and reveals a band on his wrist. He slips it off and hands it across the table. 'It does all the stuff the old pedometer used to do, plus tracks your sleep, logs your workouts and your food and water consumption. All comes straight up on your phone.'

Ewan fiddles with the gadget. 'Neat,' he says. He passes it back to his father, tucks a stray lock of hair behind his ear and smears butter on another slice of toast.

'And does it talk to you, Randal, and give you bits of well-meaning advice?' I ask.

'It does, actually. Don't mock. It analyses the data and makes recommendations.'

'"Less meat, fish, bird, egg, cheese, beans, nuts and sitting,"' I intone.

'These little information cards pop up in my UP news stream. I find them useful.' Randal slips the band over his wrist.

'Don't you remember Stanley Green and his sandwich boards in Oxford Street? I miss him. And the Hari Krishna people. Are they still there?'

I do not know why I am trying to insinuate myself into this conversation.

'Nutter, wasn't he?' Randal says.

'He wanted us all to be better, kinder, happier people. I suppose that is a type of madness. He wrote piles of letters to the government, and a novel that was never published. He lived in the house he was born in until his parents died.'

268

'There you go then. Classic indicators of derangement.'

'His book was called *Behind the Veil*.' I glance at Ewan but he is not listening. He has absented himself mentally as he and his brothers do when Randal and I are talking. Ewan will not live at home for ever, as the late Stanley Green did. It will not have occurred to him that this might be his future. It is a fear of mine because I see no way out unless through some kind of disaster that might already have happened. Two brothers live at 10 Dairyman's Road until one Cains the Abel. I, like Jean Lupton, Deborah's mother-in-law, take the role of nervous lodger.

We were never a family that did everything together – each of us was inclined to wander off – but we functioned. Day-to-day life – meals and so on – bound us. Growing up is a stop-start process that allows all parties to adjust, though there are also decisive partings, giant steps away from home and, in Ewan's case, back again. He was calm when he returned, having abandoned university – a lifeless calm.

He was an anxious little boy. Oliver and Ross were more placid. Often at bedtime Ewan asked me questions about a person or creature we had encountered – the man who trundled a bicycle laden with bags full of rubbish or a bird that would not stop cheeping. I had to rack my brain to think what he referred to. 'Is that man/bird all right?' With him, worry and vitality came roped together. A house further down Dairyman's Road he insisted was a prison. He would single out a particular black puddle, a charity volunteer dressed up in a panda suit; one winter, it was snow falling. It's snow, I said. You'll love it once we're outside. Or, It's a house like ours. The windows are metal. Their name is Crittall – and never added the phrase, Nothing to be frightened of, because words have power to make anything real. When Oliver came along he seemed to grow out of the trouble. Babies stop the world from slipping about. Day and night are alike to them, as are objects in their field of vision.

I guessed a girlfriend was the reason for his sudden retreat – or a boyfriend, or his father, or despair. I asked questions and got no answers. I was still finding my way after Randal's departure. I don't remember much about that time.

Ewan had lighter days. His face cleared. He talked with normal inflections. He went out with friends. Once, he asked to borrow money to pay for a trip to Berlin. He left his bag on the shuttle bus from Luton airport and in the hassle to retrieve it I lost the moment to find out if he had enjoyed himself. There was often – looking back – a glitch of that kind to break a good spell. That was his one trip and the only night he spent away from home until yesterday. I went up to his room before I went to bed. The roof window was open, letting in a draught of cool air. It was the same in the morning – but daylight.

55

There is a competitiveness thing going on with his son and a bit of boasting but nothing too aggressive. Randal is still sermonising about apps. I suppose his home appliances are all Web connected and he spends spare moments in his working day switching lights on or off, regulating the central heating and testing the burglar alarm. Tiresome for the nanny. If I have a complaint against new technology it is that it plays straight into the fantasies of men. Machines, a need to control, fiddling. These are my three waymarks to world meltdown. The first time I heard the words 'search engine' I knew what we were in for.

I have never been party to the father-son conversations up in the loft room. I assume they both made some kind of effort. I guessed from what Randal said and did not say and from the look on his face when he came back down that the encounters were tolerable but not easy. The strangeness of Randal calling on our eldest son in his room as though he were in a private hospital unnerved me. Summoning Ewan down to see his father would have been equally odd – and would he have appeared?

The men slouch, round-shouldered. Randal leans on his elbows and Ewan puts weight on his forearms but it is basically the same posture. They take sneaky looks at each other with a deflected, checking-up kind of appraisal without making steady eye contact. Their eyes are similar, the same changeable, tarnished colour. Both of them, for the time being, tolerate the constraints of the kitchen table, their legs out of sight underneath, crammed between the table legs, their feet placed awkwardly against various heavy items, the food processor and the largest of the cast-iron casserole dishes, the toolbox and a ten-litre bag of compost that has a hole in it. Everything is wedged in like big toys in a small box.

Then Ross walks across his bedroom floor and there is a hush that lasts a couple of seconds as we remember he is up there on the other side of the ceiling, not that any of us will have forgotten him. He turns his defiant regret against himself. We all have reason to feel bruised by his presence.

Randal says he will go and talk to him again in a moment. Ewan, who has finished eating, gets up. He leaves the used plate where it is, gives a half-nod and walks towards the doorway. We hear his feet on the stairs and the click of the door at the top of the house.

'He looks pretty fresh for someone who's been running all morning,' Randal says.

'He'll have had a shower,' I say.

'Will he? Where?'

'At Jude's?'

'Really?'

'Well, yes.'

Randal clasps his hands together and rubs his thumb knuckles against his lower teeth.

'What shall I say to him?'

'To Ross?'

Randal continues with the tooth rubbing.

'Say anything. Say what you said before.'

'I'm conscious that I'm leaving you with this problem.' He pushes down on the table and stands up. He leans towards me, his hands splayed out. The stance is what I would call aggressive. I don't know what has brought this on: Ewan's abrupt departure, without the niceties; the prospect of making no impression on Ross. These are aspects of life I live with every day. I shift my chair back a fraction and look at him. I touch one of the earrings. The cheap feel of the faceted edge seems to give me strength.

'You've made my job much harder, Lorna, by being soft with them.'

'Which job?'

He straightens up. 'It's firefighting now.'

'Oh, OK.'

'This is not where I want to be.'

'Well, we all have to live together here. I do what I can.'

He is silent, then, 'The garden's very tidy.'

'Yes, I've been clearing up out there.'

'On your own?'

'Strangely enough, Randal, I don't have a gardener.'

'I'm not talking about a gardener. Get the boys to help. You shouldn't be doing all the work. This is why you have trouble. Don't give them money until they've earned it. Good behaviour equals reward.'

'Ah, like lab rats.'

'Better than queen bees. Wish me luck.'

'I do.'

Randal turns and walks purposefully across the room. He moves like a mechanical toy. I pick up Ewan's used plate and put it in the dishwasher. I return the butter to the fridge. A packet of butter can get into a disgusting state. It starts off a nice neat brick enclosed in its wrapper and becomes deformed; an unappetising, smeared mess, infested with specks. Through the ceiling I hear Randal talking. I turn the radio on. The presenter's voice is soothing.

Miles Davis up next on *Jazz Record Requests* – and then the trumpet; a long desolate cry that prises day from night. I stretch my arms high above my head.

275

56

I walk to Winchmore Hill to visit my father. It is an anchor.

'Ground floor. Doors opening . . . sixth floor. Doors opening,' the female voice intones. The lift doors close behind me. I go along the corridor and let myself into the apartment.

'You enjoyed the walk, I expect?' my father says. He is alone.

The day is dull. The sun has not broken through. It drizzled at one point and I put up my umbrella. I do not know why I should have enjoyed the walk – and then I remember.

'Oh God, Dad, I forgot. I didn't come through the park. How could I have done that?' My hands leap to my face and press against my cheeks.

'It's not that bad,' William says.

'I love those walks. I've missed the beginning of spring. There's a bit of me that thinks the park gates have opened just for me. Magical.'

'It's quite straightforward, Lorna. Greenwich plus one.

Have you been on the wrong clock all week? I wish you'd sit down.' My father smiles. 'You used to drive your brother nuts. Subtracting when you should have been adding. And vice versa in the autumn.' He pats my hand when I settle on the arm of his chair. 'You've still got next week to enjoy the park. And then the whole of the summer. Anything new to report?'

'No.'

'Remind me of the date of Ewan's birthday. I used it as a password and I'm buggered if I can remember it.'

'The twenty-seventh of May.'

'How are the boys?'

'They're fine. Oliver's gone off to Cornwall to dive. There's just one more week of term for Ross, then it's the Easter holidays.'

William reaches for a biro and my mother's reading glasses and jots the numbers down on the top corner of the newspaper. He looks up at me. 'I wish you didn't have to deal with all this on your own, Lorna.'

'It's OK.'

57

Gervase Lupton stands up. 'On behalf of all of us present, I should like to say a big thank-you to Miss Parry for giving us such an insightful talk. I came with the preconception that archiving was boring – but far from it! The whole question of digitisation is fascinating. The first words spoken on the telephone by Alexander Graham Bell were, "Mr Watson. Come here. I need you." We know this because he very prudently made a note in his lab notebook but no one has the faintest idea what the first email said because no one bothered to document it! Mr Watson was in the next room, by the way. The extrinsic threats to anything made of paper are obvious: fire, water, mould, fungus, insect infestation. The dog ate my homework! But we don't fully comprehend the dangers to electronic data. Did you know, for example—'

'Time out,' Mrs Anstey says and raises a hand in the air.

Gervase rolls his eyes. 'We haven't clapped.'

'Go ahead,' Mrs Anstey says.

A spatter of applause follows, like a brief shower of rain on a roof.

'Thank you all for being such a lovely audience,' I say. 'And thank you, Gervase. That was a really nice speech.'

The students who attended – five girls and Gervase – are already on their feet and heading towards the door of the sixth-form common room.

'Don't leave anything behind,' Mrs Anstey calls. She slings her satchel over her shoulder.

I watch the retreating figures in black-and-white uniform.

'What did I just tell them?' Mrs Anstey points at a hairbrush and an aerosol can of deodorant under one of the grey polypropylene chairs. She switches the lights off. 'Thank you again for giving us your time. That was really very entertaining.' I can smell the woman's tapestry jacket. Eau de Oxfam, Jude called it. She was endlessly, casually cruel about the teacher's clothes. The brooches made of felt in the shape of flowers, the boiled-wool skirts. Diane Anstey will know, of course. She is no fool. She won't care what the girls think of her and her long grey hair. 'You know your way out, don't you?' Mrs Anstey smiles and ushers me through the door.

Jude, as Mrs Anstey, sat on our kitchen table. She moved from buttock to buttock to get comfortable and began to swing her legs. Slender though she is, she gave the impression of possessing a wide bottom and a large skirt. Antsy kept me behind after the lesson, Jude said. She asked if I meet up with any of the girls outside school. I said, She's a nice woman. 'You look a bit peaky. I hope you're not "on Facebook" far into the night.' Jude's imitation was scornful. *Are* the girls unkind to you? I asked. 'They're a cliquey lot but they are beginning to thaw, aren't they? Some cohorts are worse than others for bitching.' Mrs Anstey will know, I said. She's had years of experience. 'Well, if it's a boy, you are spared hours in Primark.' Jude sighed Mrs Anstey's sigh of mock exasperation. 'Get along and have your lunch. I'm looking forward to mine. A nice pork sandwich made from last night's roast dinner. Bob Anstey does all the cooking.' Jude slung the imaginary satchel over her shoulder. She gathered up the imaginary books and ring-binder of notes. She stretched out her arms, one up, one to the side, like a lollipop lady. 'Out you come, my love. Get weaving. I'm going to lock up.' Ross shuffled from foot to foot through the performance. He glanced at Jude from under his hair, captivated, and appalled by the time she wasted with me. He longed to get her back upstairs but she wasn't ready to go. Lorna, that thing you said about your friend Yorick, liking to be shut up in small spaces . . . Jude began. I've already told you. Erotic asphyxiation, Ross cut in. *Did* I say that? Chris Orrick wasn't a friend, darling. He was a member of the public. Being shut in is erotic? I don't get it, Jude said. It's not some mild spatial preference, Ross snapped back. What would be the point in that? He listed the paraphernalia that might be involved. Lorna, is it, like, widespread? Jude ventured. Don't ask her, Ross said scornfully. She doesn't know anything. Basically, you have to be a loser. They swivelled eyes at each other, secure in their plain desires.

I hear the click of the key in the lock; Mrs Anstey's footsteps retreating. The classrooms I pass are deserted. They look as though they have been targeted by a weapon that wipes out human beings, whooshes chairs to an upturned position on tables and leaves a trail of detritus; ties, blazers, scarves, shirts, football boots, A4 paper stamped with footprints or screwed into balls, pens, pencils, crisp packets, sweet wrappers, apple cores, soft-drink cans, banana skins and half-eaten filled rolls. The desolation is palpable, and the silence – though someone in an upper room plays the same phrase repeatedly on a recorder.

I finally find an exit; a door that is hanging off its hinges and partly blocked by industrial-sized bins. As I walk through the school car park, I feel something like nostalgia for the ugly collection of buildings behind me. I assumed that I would feel nothing but relief at seeing them for the last time.

58

'How was your talk?' Richard asks.

'Oh, it was fine. They were sweet, really. Mary de Silva wasn't there, although she was the one who fixed it up. Mrs Anstey, who *was* there, never mentioned her. I'm not sure Mary de Silva exists. Her manifestations are semi-miraculous. I should organise a pilgrimage to the sites where she's appeared.'

Richard Watson and I are lying on his bed. One curtain is drawn, one open. The type of fabric you might find in a hotel but we are not in a hotel. Mottled background with lozenges. The prosaic light of afternoon fills the room. Through the window, ajar at the top, I hear cars pull up and cars drive off. SUVs with bull bars front and back. Tyres scrape, doors slam. There is a pre-prep school further up the street. The boys wear St Custard's style uniform. Caps with badge, blazers with badge, short trousers, long socks.

'Off they go to their second homes for the holidays, the little beasts. I was scared.'

'Why?'

'I thought they might turn on me. Jeer at Ross. Mutter threats under their breath. But it wasn't like that. They listened and smiled at my feeble jokes. I was introduced as Lorna Parry. They might not have made a connection with Ross. Gervase Lupton is the only one who knows me – and he's pretty self-absorbed. Oh, I called Dirk Neerhoff.'

'And what did he say?'

'Frances has left with her handsome doctor. I think it's for real this time. Poor Jude. Dirk wants us to meet up.'

'Will you?'

'Are you worried? I haven't fixed a date. I might glean a little information though I expect he'll just talk about Frances. I did find out something. He drove Ewan and Jude to Northaw Woods for their run on Saturday morning. And picked them up again afterwards.'

'Oh, for Christ's sake.'

'I know. Spoon-fed.'

I am on the inner side of a bed that is pressed up against books. They fill the wall from floor to ceiling and are mostly biographies and memoirs, wide as tombstones. I have never spent the night here. Richard kindly listens to me. I soon realised that he has a low tolerance for home reportage and little interest in the young. I edit accordingly which is good discipline for me as it stops me from splurging, or offloading as people say these days.

I lop off different parts of a story according to the listener. With Richard, I confine myself to the known because he is quickly bored by supposition and I find it restful to spare myself what might be and what might have been. He laughed heartily when I told him about Ross's malicious communication. He said that Ross had added a cheering gloss to an otherwise pitiful tale and that he wouldn't at all object to being falsely remembered in black net stockings. Better than the truth, he said. This was all quite refreshing for me. Richard was brought up Roman Catholic and taught by monks. I think I can see where he is coming from.

I recall Miss Virabyan who taught drama at my old school; a subject, along with dance, that has been struck from the curriculum at Lloyd-Barron Academy. After an evening performance of *A Town like Alice* directed by Miss Virabyan, a man with an owlish expression and a full beard came up to her. He lunged and kissed her. It was not much more than a peck on the lips, fattened up by the force with which he ran into her, but, hyped up with the excitement of having been on stage, my friends and I soon turned it into a sloppy, face-eating kind of kiss and had the beard rummaging in every part of Miss Virabyan. Her hair was a true black and her skin pale as milk against the purple silk shirt that she wore on special occasions. Day after day, we embellished the story,

284

transforming it into a sexy, yucky soap opera, more compelling than anything we produced for English homework. Our silliness had no afterlife – which was a matter of good luck. Liz Savaris and I went to school in an innocent decade. We were part of the oral tradition. It was still about memory.

I could ask Liz if she remembered the bearded-lover saga but the story is dead. Miss Virabyan overheard her own name among giggles. No harm done.

I prop myself up on my elbows. The sheet that covered me slips down. From this position, I view the red bricks of the mansion block opposite that clash with the curtains. A taxi passes. The road is peaceful again. The schoolchildren have gone home.

'Are you leaving?' Richard asks.

'Yup. Better be off. See what they're up to.'

59

Some essence of Ewan remains, together with an absence as clear edged as the outline of the furniture against the white walls. The eaves slope steeply, restricting the usable space. To the left and partly under the slope is a low divan bed; to the right, a rectangular Formica table in use as a desk. The scene disconcerts me. It is as if I have stepped into a mock-up room in a museum of domestic life that is not quite right. I have seen it too often. A closed laptop, a pile of jotter pads, pots of pens and pencils, a halogen lamp angled so low that, like a heavy head, it almost hits the table. But the detail is overdone; two mugs contain residues of coffee, a fork is encrusted with something sticky, the teaspoons are stained. The first sheet of the top jotter pad is blank, and the second, though the underlying design shows dimly through. The third is a drawing I know well; the thin paper so minutely worked over in biro that its surface is twilled and ribbed like a shiny textile. The intricacy of the marks on the paper is shocking. A hundred different kinds have been used, each as meticulously replicated as embroidery stitches on a piece of fine cloth. But this is not fine cloth; it is the cheapest kind of paper and the drawing implements, the most basic ballpoint pens – the kind my father uses for the crossword puzzle. They stand in a pot on Ewan's table, bronze tipped, clear sided with the ink visible as blood in a cannula, in the standard colours of black, blue and red. So much time and effort has been spent using throwaway products. The discrepancy is a giant V-sign to something or someone. I recognise an act of undermining. The artist desperately seeks disapproval.

Alan Child is half in, half out of the door of the former walk-in stationery cupboard on the first floor of Lloyd-Barron Academy. Jude Bennet-Neerhoff aims her phone at him for the first time. He carries a grey plastic chair with metal legs. On his back is a small rucksack. The shot is not clear. He wears, in my mind's eye, the slippery lightweight jacket he had on when I met him at the sixth-form do in September. He was standing by the projector with his back to the film that no one was watching. I introduced myself. Lorna Parry, Ross Doig's mum. Parents and teachers circled around, downing the wine and, by then, showed signs of inebriation. It was dark outside and the overhead lights were on. Drink had been spilled on the carpet and crisps dropped and trodden into fragments. Noise levels were high. The atmosphere in the room had become both cosier and more rancid. I could tell he was ineffective. He lacked star teacher quality, the magnetism that is close to sexual allure and can occur in people you would never fall in love with. I just hoped he would be reasonably competent. His hand was damp and grasped mine in the wrong place so that my rings crunched together. He leant forward to speak, as we were up against a group of mouthy girls, and said – quite loudly in my ear – Are you going to tell me how wonderful Miss Bhimji was? Oh dear, I said, have you had to put up with that? The students have to try too, you know, Alan Child said. It's not just down to the teacher. Ross might as well not be there. He catches up on his sleep, he makes no contribution whatsoever and then five minutes before the hooter goes, it's all – So what was the essay title, sir? This Alan Child glossed with a silly sing-song. Clearly, he was no mimic. I'm glad to hear Ross is polite, I said. You know, it's only the second week of term. He's probably still in holiday mode. Mr Child took a step back into the beam of the projector and for a moment, a white school shirt and striped tie flickered over his face. I'm on your son's side, Mrs Doig, he said. He was hurt. Praise and complaint are the currency at school events; all of them – pupils, teachers, parents alike – want to hear how well they are doing. I felt suddenly old. I had cornered him and he, perhaps having been trapped several times by raptorial mothers and fathers eager to quiz him, had decided to land the first blow. He was too young and too inexperienced to have grasped the partisan nature of parenthood.

I hesitated, choosing between walking away and trying to make a bad situation slightly better. I looked past one of Mr Child's flexing shoulders and caught sight of Ross sidling between the art-display boards. I waved, trying to signal discreetly that I was ready to leave. He pretended not to see me. Are you coping, man? Hunter called out. Your mum wants you. He grinned, though his mouth was stuffed with a sandwich. Ross jabbed a finger upwards, in a fuck-you sign, that he modified into an upturned claw. He mouthed that he would meet me in the car park and disappeared. I apologised to Mr Child for the interruption. I was tired but I put on a bright voice. I asked him about the summer holidays. He had not done anything much, it turned out, and neither had I. He seemed to relax a little. I told him that Ross had travelled to Spain with a friend and that my middle son had gone diving. I said I did not go away because I was worried about leaving my eldest son on his own. I said I liked London in August. People drift off, the shadows grow longer and everything slows down. I don't know why I mentioned Ewan. Normally, I will not speak of him. Alan Child looked physically quite different, but something about him reminded me of my eldest son. I should be trying to make him smile, I thought. His more engaging qualities might emerge. But I ploughed on. It's not just holidays, I said. Every day when I go to work I worry and I don't know what I'll find when I get home. Alan Child said his mum had pestered him to get a job and he'd got one but that wasn't enough. 'Is it a friendly school?' He put on a well-meaning voice that was more convincing than his imitation of Ross. He said she kept asking if he liked any of the teachers. *Women* teachers. She didn't understand about pressure. While he talked, his eyes met mine, as though he had bumped into me. He paused. His gaze veered off. It was strange, in school, to be having a real conversation. Both of us disclosed our anxious thoughts. We talked for about twenty minutes and then Simon Petridis came up, determined to discuss Evie: My daughter had excellent reports from your predecessor and of course the A star at GCSE . . .

I told Alan Child that I'd enjoyed speaking to him. As I turned to go – Simon still talking away – he touched my arm. I expect he'll be all right – your son Ewan, he said.

I walked on past when I saw him by the lake in Grovelands Park.

He flicks the light switch to make sure it is in the 'off' position. Leaving the door ajar, he places the chair in the centre of the floor, opens the rucksack and takes out a light bulb still in its box. Children's voices echo in the well of the stairs and feet clatter in ascending and descending scales. In semi-darkness, he removes the packaging and climbs onto the chair, holding the bulb aloft by its glass. The unused cupboard retains the dry smell of old paper. The sturdy wooden shelves that go from floor to ceiling are empty but for a scattering of treasury tags and a single bulldog clip; obsolete items from the era of stationery, later captured by Jude Bennet-Neerhoff in a series of stills. Neatly stacked exercise books with chalky coloured covers have gone and never been replaced. Thousands of them. Red for history, blue for English, with square-crossed pages for maths and with printed bar lines for music, rough books made of coarse paper, little notebooks for vocab. Each one was a new start. A Grundig reel-to-reel tape recorder stands in a corner. It is as sturdy as a piece of military equipment, with its grey box top, and Alan has it marked down as an additional aid if he fails to reach the ceiling. Finding the stationery cupboard has been a godsend. The last thing he wants is to make a spectacle of himself by changing into his cycling gear in an ostentatious manner and setting off in full view of the staffroom window. The sports department is always on the lookout for semi-fit volunteers who can be dragged onto the football pitch or basketball court. By stretching up into dusty space, he manages to reach the light fitting. He gets off the chair and presses the switch. The room is illuminated. Through the wall he hears a ball bounce down the stairs and children yelling as they pursue it.

The second shot of Alan Child entering the stationery cupboard also features a chair and a rucksack, though this time he drags the chair. Jude Bennet-Neerhoff aims her phone at him. The door shuts.

If Alan's mother imagined him in the staffroom, nursing a mug of instant coffee, somewhat on the edge of things, not part of a bitching faction but conversing in an intelligent way with like-minded colleagues, she was wrong. He started out that way and was now in flight, not during lessons or when obliged to do duties, but in those narrow bands of time that are, occasionally, his own.

Alan pulls his phone out of his pocket and checks the time. Twelve-forty. He has a good half-hour before he needs to be back for the first lesson of the afternoon and no lunch-time duties on a Friday. He slips off the rucksack, dips into it and produces a few tools, a wire coat hanger and a rope. He ascends the ladder again and drills a hole through the top shelf with a hand drill. He descends. He unties the laces of his black leather shoes. His actions are quick. Jacket, tie, shirt, belt, trousers; the teacher's clothes come off and are arranged over the

292

hanger. He is off for a long bike ride. It will get him away from school and clear his head. That option remains open to him until he chooses the other one. Once he is down to his underpants, he rapidly pulls on a pair of tracksuit bottoms and zips up the matching top. Trainers on, laces tied; he is ready to go.

One of Randal's light-bulb jokes.

60

He has his art, maybe that will lead somewhere, Randal said, early on. The alphabet in biro. I don't think so, I said.

I examine again the everyday objects, buildings, plants, creatures, the luminous band of asteroids in a black sky, made from marks tiny as pixilation, and, staring further into them, I try to see the letter that they begin with – the letter 'A'– that I know covers the whole page and is concealed in the design. I switch on the lamp, kneel down and put my nose close to the paper. My head is bowed, the soles of my feet upturned. I used to make paper boats for Ewan. He sailed them in the bath.

The event I feared has happened – though to another mother's son. It occupied a corner of my mind, pitched a small tent there. A ridge-framed object, flap closed, sleeps one. Not a refuge. We all contributed to the offence against Mr Child. It doesn't much matter who pressed 'send'. Jude took the photos and got away with it. She has taken Ewan too. No help to Ross in his trouble. I am years behind with the products of technology. I read about things like Google-Glass and think, for God's sake. Why would anyone want to wear a headset that connects to the Internet? The next thing will be smart contact lenses and implants in the eyes because swiping and tapping a pair of goggles is a giveaway. People take pictures of everything. The subject has no significance. Whatever comes by is reflected. A picture on a phone; it's what they do. If I were into that kind of thing, I would have taken one of my ex-husband appraising Jude's breasts. What used to be lost is now preserved; trash, that is. Preserved and multiplied.

Slowly, I move in and out, near and away. The knack of finding the initial letter hidden in the design is to de-couple the two types of looking, the gaze and the focus, but the point where the trick works eludes me. I go for another approach, an ad-hoc type of geometry that locates the notional apex of a triangle at the top mid-point and traces imagined sides. *Isos*, equal, and *skelos*, leg. I envisage a cross-bar and the angle of the A's smaller triangle. I search for a pattern behind the pattern – or an angel that would fit on a shirt button. My youngest son crosses his room with thumping footsteps. Then his music comes on. If he remains pig-headed, I shall have to help him find somewhere else to continue his education. Life in the summer is easier – light for longer in the evening – though too hot here under the roof. There is nothing but sky above the slanting window. Half-remembering, half-dreaming, I hear my own mother's voice. It comes from a long way back, before I grew up, before I was born; the mother as mainstay infinitely regressing, turning into smaller and smaller copies of herself and bequeathing a diminishing feeling of safety.

penguin.co.uk/vintage